MISSION TYPHOON

This edition published in 2016 by Ipso Books

Ipso Books is a division of Peters Fraser + Dunlop Ltd

Drury House, 34-43 Russell Street, London WC2B 5HA

To Scouts all over the world – part of a family some 40 million strong. Bound together by a love of adventure and friendships that last a lifetime.

Respect to you all.

CHARACTER PROFILES

Beck Granger

Beck Granger is just fourteen but knows more about the art of survival than most adults learn in a lifetime. As a small child, he picked up many traditional survival skills from the remote tribes around the world that his parents stayed with. Since then he has practiced and honed his abilities in tropical jungles, arid deserts and frozen wastelands all over the globe.

Li Ju-Long

Thirteen-year-old Ju-Long has badges of excellence from her Young Pioneers battalion for sports that include camping, climbing, sailing and swimming, and so she feels ready for anything that a simple hiking expedition can throw at her. Even when things turn out markedly different to her expectations, she is a fast learner and it soon seems that there are even other skills that she can teach Beck.

Mr Zhou

A passionate and experienced sportsman, Mr Zhou is also calm, capable and brave, and the natural leader for an outward bound expedition. He will do anything to protect the young people in his care, even to the extent of putting his own life in danger.

MISSION TYPHOON

BEAR GRYLLS

ipso books

CHAPTER 1

Beneath the regular thudding of the blades, Beck Granger felt the helicopter lurch. He glanced out of the window at the thickly forested hills of southern China's Guangxi province. There was no question about it. They had changed course, and they were losing speed.

Beck and the Chinese girl sitting next to him looked at each other and checked their watches. Ju-Long looked as surprised as he felt.

"It is too soon," she agreed. They were due to fly for another half hour before the helicopter dropped them off. And if there was a change of plan, Beck thought, they should both have been told about it. They had a right to be informed. They were Junior Leaders, second in command to the two adult men in charge of the expedition. The idea was to train them up to lead youth treks in their own right.

"Yay! We're landing!" someone behind them called. The passenger cabin filled with cheers. It was mostly full of teenagers, twenty of them, half Chinese and half from Europe, Australia and New Zealand.

Beck didn't cheer. He felt his guts tighten inside him. He had been on a light aircraft once before that had suddenly developed engine trouble in the middle of the wilderness. It had crashed and the pilot had been killed. He had then had to trek over the mountains of Alaska with a friend to get help for his seriously injured uncle. He *really* hoped this trip wasn't going the same way...

The trees four hundred feet below were like a rumpled carpet of thick green velvet. A river gorge cut through the overgrown landscape like a deep slash. Down at the bottom, even from up here, Beck could see where rapids and rocks churned the water into white foam. It must be a fierce torrent, which over the years had sliced its way deep through the heart of the rocks around it.

Even if it wasn't like the rain forest, where Beck had been before – with giant trees twenty or thirty metres high, and multiple canopies of leaves and branches that blocked out the sky – Beck knew it was still proper jungle down there. It was a tropical forest, thick, wild and untamed. These trees would be smaller than in the rain forest, packed closer together, with the canopy nearer the ground. It would make trekking through them all the more difficult.

Well, it was never meant to be *easy*. It just wasn't meant to be *now*.

But, as far as his ears could tell, there was nothing wrong with the engines. The change of course and height must be deliberate. Perhaps the leaders had planned a surprise for them.

And if there was one thing Beck hated on a well-planned expedition, it was surprises. He knew how to handle them, and that knowledge had saved his life on many occasions. And that was exactly why he knew you shouldn't go out looking for them.

"Attention! Attention please!"

The two adult leaders of the expedition, Mr Zhou and Mr Muller, had stood up at the front of the cabin. Mr Muller, the senior of the two, had the microphone so that everyone could hear him over the noise of the engines. He was a German man in his thirties, with close cropped hair and a big smile.

"There has been a change of plan!"

Somehow he managed to make it sound like the best news ever. Whenever Beck thought of him, he pictured a man bouncing up and down on his toes with excitement, even if he was just ordering a coffee.

"Perhaps you have been following Typhoon Liling in the news, *ja*? It is raging on the south coast. When we planned this expedition, all the reports said that Liling would safely miss us. Since then the experts have had to change their assessment. Liling has swerved beyond its expected course."

No one was cheering in the cabin now. Beck shot a look again out of the window. The sky was certainly dark and overcast. So, there was a typhoon coming? Winds of over 100 miles per hour, five feet of rain falling in twenty four hours? They must be cancelling the trek. That was a shame, but it was the sensible thing to do.

"But," Mr Muller said with a grin, "it will not *quite* hit us. Not with all its strength. We will notice its effects on the edges. So, we are landing early, short of our intended destination – it will soon not be safe for the pilot to fly – and we will trek through the jungle to a sheltered area where we will wait for the storm to pass. Then we will make our way to the planned route through the national park."

Eh? Beck couldn't quite believe his ears. How was that the sensible thing to do? He could see that Mr Zhou, a grizzled Chinese man, felt uncertain – but, Mr Muller was the senior leader.

"There is a clearing ten minutes away where the pilot will put us down. Start preparing now."

Mr Muller hung the microphone up and bent his head to talk to Mr Zhou.

Beck was up and out of his seat.

"Excuse me, Mr Muller, sir?"

The leader shot him a look that barely hid annoyance.

"Yes, Beck, what is it?"

"Sir," Beck said, "with respect, if the typhoon is coming anywhere near us, we should go back to base and wait for it to pass."

"It is what I have been saying..." Mr Zhou joined in. Mr Muller cut them both off.

"Yes, yes, all this has been considered. No one wants to cancel this expedition, do they?"

He put gentle hands on Beck's shoulders and turned him to face the cabin.

"You see all those happy faces, Beck? How everyone is looking forward to this? And we are at the start of a whole new venture. New ideas that do not quickly take root are quickly cut down."

Beck shrugged his hands off as politely as he could and turned back to face him. He understood the politics of the situation. He also understood that danger doesn't care about politics. He opened his mouth to speak, but Mr Muller got in there first.

"So, this is a compromise. Perhaps we will get a little wet but that is the point of a venture like this." He shot Beck a sly sideways look. "And anyway, Beck, are you not the survival expert?"

Beck felt himself flush, but he let it pass.

"I might know a thing or two, sir," he said, "but one of the main things to know about survival is not to get into those situations in the first place if you can help it. If the typhoon's changed course once, it can change again, and we'll be stuck on the ground –"

Mr Muller cut him off with an abrupt gesture.

"Thank you, Beck, we are all familiar with your expertise. Perhaps you can try to remember there are other people who also know what they are doing, ja? Perhaps your uncle is in charge of the organisation but I am in charge of this expedition. Now, sit down and prepare for disembarking."

Beck went back to his seat with his ears flaming. Ju-Long had been too far back to hear the conversation. She shot him a puzzled look but he didn't return it. His thoughts were too taken up with Mr Muller.

What an idiot!

Yes, Beck had a certain reputation as a survival expert. Mr Muller was right about that. He hadn't asked for it. He had never wanted to be famous – it just followed him around. And he had to admit he hadn't exactly made it easy for himself. Recently, for very good reasons, he had had to fake his own death. It had made the headlines. It had made even more headlines when the world learned that he was still alive. He had managed to bring down a corrupt businessman and make the world a slightly better place, so he wasn't ashamed of what he had done.

There had been a cost, and it still made his toes curl when he thought about it. Samora, the South African girl who had befriended him, hadn't spoken to him since. And he could only imagine how much he had hurt Uncle Al, who had raised him like a son.

But now the Mr Mullers of this world had him pegged as a troublemaker, and they never passed up the opportunity to remind him of it.

Beck had seen an opportunity and he had taken it. It had occurred to him, many times since, that perhaps he could have thought about it a bit more. Over-enthusiasm could cloud the mind as much as fear, with similar effects.

"What was that about?" Ju-Long asked.

"Tell you later," Beck said through his teeth. He pulled his backpack down from the rack and started to go through it.

Okay, so Mr Muller was going to do this and no one could stop him. That made it even more important that Beck could lend his expertise where it was going to be needed.

Because, deliberately landing anywhere near a typhoon, even on the edges, was never going to be a good idea.

CHAPTER 2

Two days earlier

"You must be Beck Granger –"

"You must be Li Ju-Long…"

Beck and Ju-Long smiled at each other. Beck found himself looking at a slim Chinese girl of about his own age. Like all the Chinese girls and boys in the room, she wore the uniform of the Young Pioneers: light blue trousers, a white top and a red scarf.

The hotel room was full of young people from different nations, slowly starting to chat with each other. This was officially Day One of the trek, or possibly Day Zero. Most of the party were meeting today for the first time – ten Young Pioneers from China and ten young people from similar organisations in other countries. And Beck. This get-together in a Hong Kong hotel was their chance to learn each other's names and be briefed for what lay ahead.

Their hosts had gone out of their way to make everyone welcome. They had laid on a traditional Chinese dragon dance outside the hotel – people had laughed and clapped as a thirty metre dragon swooped and curled its way through the crowd, guided by the performers inside it. Now, the room was festooned with banners, music played in the background, and the tables were laid with about a million delicious little nibbles.

Everyone had been a little nervous at first, no one quite talking to each other. Mr Zhou and Mr Muller had got round that by putting everyone into pairs, a Chinese and a non-Chinese together. They each got a badge with the other person's name on, and had to wander around until they found their own name stuck onto someone else. Now the background buzz was slowly growing.

Beck had been circulating, trying to find Ju-Long, but his attention had been caught by a TV screen on a small stage at one end of the room. It was tuned to a running news channel, and the typhoon was the main item of interest. He had heard the day before that it had hit the Philippines, a few hundred kilometres to the south. Footage of storm-lashed seas and trees whipping back and forth, combined with satellite photos and graphics, made it very clear that the islands were getting it very hard from storm force winds. He watched gravely, feeling a little guilty that he was pleased not to be there. There would be thousands of people homeless after this.

And then Ju-Long found him, and he pushed it to the back of his mind. As Ju-Long and Beck were the Junior Leaders, it made sense that they had been put together. They were expected to learn from each other, as well as the adults, so that they could pass on their skills to the less experienced kids under them.

"Ah! You've found each other. Excellent."

Mr Muller had come up behind them. He gave them both a pat on the shoulder, then leaned close to Ju-Long and spoke in a stage whisper.

"Be nice to him! He's related to the boss!" He flashed them a friendly smile and disappeared into the crowd, while Beck closed his eyes and groaned inside.

She looked after him, then turned eyes back to Beck that were friendly but puzzled.

"Was he making a joke?"

Beck grunted.

"He was trying."

Her English was very good – though even very bad English would have been better than his non-existent grasp of Standard Chinese.

"And are you related ..."

"To the boss? No." IYTO, the International Youth Trekking Organisation, didn't have a boss. It was run by a committee. Honesty made Beck add: "But my Uncle Al is one of the founders. It's a cause he really believes in – helping young people around the world get to know and understand each other better."

Al's thinking was simple. *If they can get to know and trust and like each other,* he would say, *then, when they grow up, half the barriers that exist between the adults of different countries will have been erased at a stroke.*

"He sounds a very wise man," Ju-Long said, and she smiled, so Beck guessed she was not just being polite. He smiled back.

"Thanks. I think so."

Though sometimes Beck wondered if Al hadn't had another reason to get involved with IYTO ...

Beck's parents had worked for the environmental action group Green Force. It provided money and support to causes around the world. Beck was hugely proud of what they had achieved in their lifetimes, even though it had made them many enemies and ultimately got them killed. Beck had lived with Al since he was little, and he had made no secret of the fact that one day he wanted to work for Green Force too.

Soon after his latest adventures, in Africa and Nepal, when he had been forced to fake his own death to help him confront Green Force's worst enemy, Al had come up with the idea of IYTO. Beck had a strong suspicion that it was meant to be a diversion. Al wanted to distract Beck from more dangerous pursuits and keep him out of trouble. If it helped other young people too, that was just gravy.

With the adventures Beck had been having in recent years, accidental and deliberate, he could understand if Al felt that way. And he appreciated the effort. He also already knew it wasn't going to work – he cared too much for what Green Force did – but he could afford to relax a little, and so far IYTO was helping him do that. Maybe it was all a lot tamer than some of the stuff he had done, but that also suited him just fine.

He decided to change the subject.

"This is my first time in China. I'm looking forward to finding out about it."

She laughed.

"Well, it is my first time this far south. My mother is a factory manager in Wuhan and my father is an office administrator. So we are both learning. I know this is the first IYTO expedition, but if you are a Junior Leader, I take it you are experienced in this kind of thing already?"

She asked the question brightly and Beck took a moment to look carefully at her. No, she wasn't joking. She had never heard of him before today. Compared with some of his experiences back home – chat shows asking intrusive questions, photographers with long range lenses determined to catch him doing something, anything – it was like a drink of cool, fresh water. He looked forward to being friends with Ju-Long and all the Chinese, based only on the adventures they were going to share together.

"I've done a bit," he admitted. "You?"

"Oh, I have been doing outdoor activities for as long as I can remember," she said proudly. "I have badges of excellence from the Young Pioneers for hiking, camping, climbing, sailing and swimming."

"Ah." Beck bit his lip. "I – uh – don't actually have any badges for anything."

She frowned, a little. "But you are experienced?"

"Oh ... yes. Only, I tended to learn it all on the job. They don't actually give badges for what I'm good at."

"Which is?"

"Um ..." Beck shrugged. "Survival."

It wasn't meant to have been that way. It was just that his parents, travelling the world with Green Force, had always made sure that the locals could teach him their ways – ways that had helped their people stay alive for thousands of years before western civilisation caught up with them. In modern terms, that translated into survival.

"I see ... But we should have no need for survival skills on this trip."

"Well, exactly," he agreed. "You *should* never need survival skills at all, because everything *should* go to plan. But it's handy to have those skills when it doesn't."

He hoped he wasn't coming across too heavy. She paused a moment, then shook his hand.

"Well, Beck Granger, I am looking forward to working with you." Her smile was genuine and friendly. He had no difficulty returning it.

"Thank you. Likewise."

"Attention! Your attention please!"

Mr Muller and Mr Zhou had gone up onto a small stage at one end of the room. Mr Muller clapped his hands together a couple of times to ensure everyone was looking. He continued, beaming his smile around the room.

"I hope you are all getting to know each other well. There will be more opportunities over dinner and in the days ahead."

Mr Zhou kept up a running translation for the non-English speakers, while Mr Muller waved a remote control. The news coverage on the screen disappeared to be replaced by a map of southern China. "Let me now tell you about the next few days. Tomorrow morning we will be picked up by a minibus and taken to the airport, where we will fly inland. Tomorrow after-noon will be spent on short treks as we get to know one another. The day after tomorrow, first thing we will rendezvous with a helicopter that will take us into the mountains, to the Guilin Li River National Park, in Guangxi Province. From there we will take existing trails for the first day, after which we will strike out across country..."

CHAPTER 3

The next day

The expedition was assembling in the hotel's reception area after a slap-up breakfast in the restaurant. Beck was pleased to see it looked like the get-together had worked. The two groups were mixing together a little more easily.

"Ju-Long! Beck!" Mr Zhou called. "We leave in five minutes. Make sure both your groups are here and have all their equipment."

Beck easily did a quick head count of his party. Yup, all here, no problem.

And then – oh. Problem. He hurried quickly over to where two of the boys and two of the girls were chatting together. They gave him a friendly wave when he came up.

"Hi, Beck!"

"Hi. Uh – guys." They picked up something from his tone and looked at him worriedly. "You can't go dressed like that."

"Huh?" They all looked down at themselves. Two of them were in shorts. The long type that came down below the knee, but even so.

"Jungles are full of biting insects, and plants that scratch," Beck said. "And even the smallest scratch can go septic, or just drive you crazy with itching. You need to keep your skin covered as much as possible. Shorts are no good. Have you got anything longer? Like this?"

He indicated his own trousers. They were made of tough, sturdy fabric that would resist most cuts and tears and protect against thorns and whipping undergrowth.

"Uh..." They looked at each other. "Yeah. In our packs."

"Well, you need to go and put them on."

There was no point being a Junior Leader, Beck reckoned, if you didn't lead. Especially when you happened to be right.

"You know we've checked out of our rooms, right? Where do we get changed?" one of them asked.

"In the restroom, Brainiac," said the other. "C'mon."

They headed quickly off. The two who were left were exchanging superior smiles, when Beck let them have it.

"And you two need to change too."

"Huh? But we're not in shorts..."

The boy gestured at his legs. They were both in trousers that were almost skin-tight. Probably very fashionable, back home.

"Yeah, and you've gone too far in the other direction," Beck told them. "They need to be loose, to let the air circulate. Otherwise you'll overheat. Your sweat won't evaporate." Again he tugged on his own trousers by way of demonstration. He always preferred trousers with built-in mesh vents that let the air circulate past his skin, carrying away excess heat and drying perspiration. "You got anything that's strong and loose?"

"Uh – yeah..." said the boy.

"C'mon," said the girl resignedly. She was already on her way to the restrooms.

Beck gave them a quick visual check as they hurried away, from the feet up. The rest of what they were wearing looked okay. Good, sturdy boots that covered the ankles and would give support on the trickiest ground. Thick socks inside them, to hold the feet firm and stop them rubbing against the leather.

On the tops of their bodies, most of the trekkers wore two or three layers like Beck – a t-shirt, a sweatshirt and a light waterproof cagoule. Again, it was all about letting the air circulate. The layers didn't block it, but at the same time, added all together they kept the wind and the rain out, and prevented the body from getting too cool.

"Clothing trouble?" Ju-Long asked, coming up to him. He gave her a rueful smile. All the Chinese on the expedition had been dressed for it properly, of course. Earning all those Young Pioneer activity badges had taught them the importance of being kitted out properly.

"Just sorting it out," he said. "It's another of those things that we *shouldn't* need – but we might."

The trek would be along trails in the jungle that had already been explored. It wasn't as if they were going into the unknown. Mr Muller and Mr Zhou had been over the maps with Beck and Ju-Long to show them the way. But Beck liked to be prepared...

... And that was why he had a couple of items on him that were all his own. In his backpack was a pocket knife – a wooden handle, with a couple of blades that folded in. The handle was shaped to fit his hand so that he could keep a good grip on it, whatever he was doing. And round his neck, dangling next to his skin, was his most prized possession of all – his new fire steel. It had been a birthday present from Uncle Al. His original fire steel, which he had had for as long as he could remember, had been lost in a shipwreck in the Bermuda Triangle. It consisted of a couple of pieces of metal, a flat square like a blunt razor blade and a short rod. The rod was made of ferrocerium, a combination of magnesium and other chemicals. When the scraper struck the rod it threw off a blaze of sparks. Beck had started more life-saving fires than he could remember with his old fire steel and he had missed it terribly. It had been about time to get a new one.

Mr Muller was doing a headcount. His habitual smile was replaced with a look of frustration.

"Beck! Several of your party are missing. I thought they were all here a moment ago ..."

"They're in the loos, Mr Muller. I told them to get changed properly."

"Beck, you are holding up the expedition!" Mr Muller said in exasperation. "They will be walking along established trails. It is not as if we will be hacking our way through primary jungle! Ah, here they come. Quickly, quickly now, into the minibus, if we have all passed Mr Granger's exacting standards for this mission ..."

Beck quietly shouldered his pack and joined the line for the minibus that would take them to the heliport.

You shouldn't have to hack your way through primary jungle, he thought. *Secondary jungle is the real problem ...*

Primary jungle was natural jungle – hundreds, maybe thousands of years old. The many forms of plant life growing there had got used to each other. They grew in a natural balance, not too far apart, not too packed. It was relatively easy for a human to get through primary jungle.

But secondary jungle was where the primary jungle had been cleared away, maybe by farmers or developers, to expose the ground. This meant the sun and rain could get down there for the first time in centuries and give all the hopeful little plants there the boost they had been waiting for. They then grew, wildly and madly together, making a thick, impenetrable barrier.

Beck guessed Mr Muller didn't know that, and that kind of worried him. Mr Muller wasn't stupid – far from it. Uncle Al had picked him for the job, after all. He was an experienced trekker, an outdoorsman since he was a boy. He had made TV shows and written articles about his experiences – all of which were in Europe. Europe didn't get much jungle, primary or secondary. Mr Muller had no experience of this part of the world. A fish out of water may be excellent at being a fish, but it's still in the wrong place.

But, Uncle Al wouldn't have given him the job if he hadn't thought Mr Muller could do it, and Beck had to trust his uncle's opinion. The expedition would be mostly sticking to established tracks, and where it wasn't, it had Mr Zhou to provide first-hand, local guidance. Beck knew a lot less about the Chinese trek leader, but what he did know, he liked. Mr Muller's inexperience in this kind of landscape oughtn't to matter.

Beck told himself that, very firmly, before stepping after the others into the minibus.

The last thing he saw as they left the reception area was the large TV screen behind the receptionists' desk. It was showing the same running news channel he had seen at the get-together. The typhoon was still blowing, and had moved closer to the mainland.

CHAPTER 4

The helicopter's engines bellowed as its rotors pushed it back off the ground on a column of air that sent a small barrage of leaves and plant debris whirling around the clearing. The trekkers flinched away and covered their faces until the frenzy had passed. They straightened up as the helicopter disappeared over the trees.

Well, here we are, Beck thought morosely. He cocked an eye up at the sky. The clouds were low and thick, moving with visible speed. The trees thrashed back and forth in the wind and set up a steady roar that dinned in his ears. The air brushing against his face was warm and moist. All the signs, he knew from experience, of a good tropical storm.

Mr Muller called everyone together. He was in the middle of a jungle on the edge of a typhoon, and he still managed to grin like a little boy who had been given an enormous treat.

"About two hour's walk from here is a cave complex. We will shelter there and wait for Liling to pass completely. Along the way we will learn from Mr Zhou about moving through jungle. Beck, Ju-Long, get your people together and make sure they are properly equipped."

As Junior Leader, Beck had already seen to that before everyone boarded the helicopter. He only needed to make a few final checks to see that everyone was dressed appropriately. He was more concerned about what was in their heads than on their bodies. Some of them looked anxious but most looked cautiously keen – the kind of enthusiasm you showed when you knew you were in for some hard work, like going on a long run or a hard climb, but it would all work out well. They had faith in the leaders, and Beck had to accept Mr Muller's argument that it was worth pressing on for their sake.

And, Mr Muller's immediate aim was to press on to a place where they could all wait safely. That showed the right sense of priorities, at least.

Mr Zhou and Mr Muller had their heads together, comparing Mr Muller's GPS with Mr Zhou's map. Eventually they came to an agreement.

"Move on!" Mr Muller called. "We will lead; Ju-Long, Beck, you bring up the rear." And so the expedition set off into the jungle.

Beck kept an eye on the faces of the girls and boys passing him by. Some showed a lively interest in what was going on around them. Some were deep in conversation with each other and didn't seem to notice anything. And some looked distinctly edgy, walking and peering around as if they expected a tiger to jump out from behind every tree.

Ju-Long herself gave him a flat smile as they fell into step at the end of the column, and he sensed her pre-occupation.

"I think some of them are feeling nervous," Beck said quietly. He didn't add, *including you*. It seemed a good way to raise the subject.

"Many of us have not been in precisely this situation," she said after a moment. In other words, Beck guessed, all the badges she had won had been hard earned, yes, but earned in controlled situations. They had never had to make an emergency trek through unexplored jungle before. Ju-Long struck him as someone who was capable and organised – which meant she preferred other things to be organised too.

"You know," he said, "a jungle is the most amazing place on the planet. There's nowhere else with so much life. But, you know, it's just a system?"

"A system?"

"Think of it like a machine. It's a big machine but it still follows rules. Water circulates – it goes from rain to the ground to plants to evaporation to rain again. And every animal has its place, here, from tiny insects to big mammals."

Animals bred, preyed, died and became food for other animals to repeat the cycle. He wouldn't make a big thing about the dying bit.

"So, all a human has to do is move with it, not fight it. We've got something no other animals have – we've got the brains and skills to use a situation and make sure we stay on top of it."

And if the worst came to the worst – something else he didn't say – Mr Zhou and Mr Muller had a radio that could call for help. But he didn't want her to be relying on the adult leaders. He wanted her to be able to face her fears based on the strength of her own understanding.

She smiled, with a bit more confidence.

"Thank you for that. I suggest we each pass it on to our teams. They may be reassured."

"Hey, I remember my first time in the jungle," he said. "My parents were working for Green Force in Borneo. We all stayed in a village in the middle of the jungle there."

Beck had found its sheer size and intensity to be terrifying when he was little and unused to it. He could still feel a little of that now, deep down, as the jungle breathed and moved in the wind around him. But the people in the Bornean village had shown him what he had told the girl – the proper way to see it. Since then he had had to survive in a jungle twice, once in Central America and once in Indonesia, and lived to tell the tale.

Ju-Long looked around.

"I have never been here before but I know my great grandparents did. They were guerrillas in the Second World War, fighting against the Japanese invaders. They could hide here quite safely."

"I can believe it," Beck said sincerely, looking around. He had seen the lie of the land from the air: the steep slopes, the dense tree coverage. Nature would have given this part of the world a million nooks and crannies. An army could hide here and not be found if it didn't want to be.

And always around them was the unseen force of Typhoon Liling, gusting through the leaves and branches. It carried the smells of a billion tons of biomass, animal and vegetable, living and dead.

And then it began to rain. Not just rain, *pour*. And pour, and pour. It started as a hissing in the tree tops, and then the drops came through, thick and heavy and warm.

Beck rolled his eyes and put his hood up. He was just glad this was the edge of the typhoon.

At least the rain was falling vertically down through the trees. If they had been out in the open, they would have been blinded by sheets of water travelling horizontally through the air. Here, the trees broke up the downpour so that it just fell on top of them.

They weren't going to get blown away by the wind. They were high up on a plateau, so there would be no sudden floods to sweep anyone away. The worst that could happen was that they all got soaked, and they all had dry clothes tucked away in their backpacks (something else that Beck had checked for each trekker).

But it was still *unnecessary*. That was what made Beck seethe. Mr Muller might be a great trek leader but he knew nothing about survival. They were two different things. The first rule for getting out of trouble was: stay out of trouble in the first place.

They had landed just before ten o'clock. They trudged through the soaking jungle for the next hour. The ground rose and fell in the shadows and hidden by the trunks. At this stage, there was no obvious path for the group to follow. They were aiming for an established track but they had to pass through raw jungle to get there, and Mr Muller was following the course dictated by the GPS, which was more or less a straight line. Unfortunately, jungles don't agree with straight lines and they make it almost impossible to stick to one. The column of trekkers twisted and wound its way through the undergrowth and Beck had the feeling they were marching twice as far, and half as fast, as they needed to.

The girl in front of Beck suddenly stumbled and almost fell. Her leg was stretched out behind her, with her foot pinned down by something. She straightened herself up and tried to jerk her foot away. She jerked again, harder. Her foot didn't move. Beck looked down and saw that her boot had got caught in a vine that looped out of the ground. The vine was no thicker than a piece of parcel string, but it was a lot stronger.

"Okay, okay." He put his hand on her shoulder. "Stop fighting it because you'll lose. Just take your foot back out of it, nice and easy."

She scowled, but she did as he had told her. Even that was easier said than done, as her struggles had just made the vine tighter. He knelt down to help her free her foot. When it was out, he took hold of the vine in both hands, wrapping it around his fingers to get a grip, and jerked as hard as he could in both directions. After several tries, he managed to make it snap.

"Never try to fight the jungle," he said with a smile. "It only fights back. Just think of that little vine, and then multiply by several billion – that's what we're up against here. And this was only a tiddler. Stronger ones, you could climb with ..."

"Beck!" Mr Muller was calling from the head of the column. Beck tried not to roll his eyes. What had he done wrong now?

CHAPTER 5

Beck made his way past the others and up to the front of the trek. He had braced himself for some new criticism from Mr Muller, so he was pleasantly surprised to find the leader was looking at his GPS in frustration, as though he was baffled by the signals it was sending out.

"Beck, you have been in the jungle before, *ja*?"

"Ja – I mean, um, yes."

"This is taking too long. We need your expertise. I will keep us on track with this, but you must find our path for us. Mr Zhou will take your place with Ju-Long at the rear."

"Um – sure, sir," Beck said in surprise. His eyes met Mr Zhou's, and he could have sworn Mr Zhou winked. Or something very like it.

Mr Zhou must have set this up. He could just as easily have lead the group from the front himself. Did he want to demonstrate to Mr Muller that Beck knew his stuff? Beck gave the man a grateful half-smile as he headed to the end of the line.

"Before we go any further…" Beck said. He pulled his knife out and hacked off a thin branch from a tree, the length and size of a walking stick. "Which way, sir?"

Mr Muller checked the GPS, then silently pointed, and Beck set off as close to the direction indicated as he could. He probed the way ahead with the stick, like a blind person might make their way along the pavement, even though he could see clearly.

And he deliberately made noise with his feet as he went. It served two purposes. First, any snakes up ahead would sense the vibrations and get out of the way. And second, if they didn't but still felt like having a go, they would strike at the stick and not his leg.

After that, their movement got a little easier. Beck would head as far as he could in a given direction, until Mr Muller gave him a correction from the GPS, and he would start off on a new course.

From his time in the jungle of Borneo as a child, and from the time he and his friend Peter had been stranded in the Indonesian jungle trying to evade illegal poachers, Beck had learned to read the land. You don't concentrate too much on the obstacles in front of you because then you won't see the bigger picture. He had been taught to look *through* the undergrowth, not at it. That way you get a sense of the contours of the land and the density of the undergrowth ahead of you. If there was a thick tangle of bushes up ahead that you would have to go around, you altered course beforehand to avoid them in the first place. If your way was blocked by a fallen trunk, you could head past it instead.

He began to call instructions back. Like the girl with her foot in a vine, you had to learn to go with what the jungle wanted, not what you wanted. So, you couldn't just walk along like you were strolling in the park.

"Duck here," he would call, or, "Swivel round..."

Eventually everyone just learned to copy his movements, bending themselves around obstacles, sliding between trunks, shortening or lengthening their stride as was needed.

The rain dried up eventually, though it was hard to tell at first. Drops the size of ping pong balls still fell through the leaves above.

And suddenly they were on a track. A small cheer went up from the front of the column. Beck thought at first that Mr Muller's navigation had actually got them to where they were meant to be, before he remembered that they were meant to get to the caves before they got to the established trail.

"Excellent!" Mr Muller squinted along the way through the leaves. "Thank you, Beck. That was very helpful."

But Beck had seen what had happened. They hadn't actually got anywhere significant.

"This is only an animal trail, though, sir," he pointed out. The track was very faint and also very narrow, just wide enough to walk in single file. Beck could see how the trail had come about. On their left, the ground rose sharply. On their right, it fell away down a steep slope. They must be high up on the side of a hill. Trees still grew out of the slope and reached above their heads, blocking the view of whatever lay below. Jungle animals had made this track, instinctively taking the easy route along this narrow strip of level ground. Every creature that came this way made it slightly easier for the next one, and before long there was a trail, plain for all to see.

"I can see that, thank you," Mr Muller said, "but it does lead in the direction we want. This way!"

Now Mr Muller was in front again, leading the way. And then, suddenly, they were out in the clear daylight.

Beck whistled.

The ground to their left was almost vertical, a sheer cliff of rock and earth. There were no trees here – there was nothing for their roots to get a hold of – so the view was unbroken.

To their right, the ground dropped 100 metres straight down. They were at the top of a river gorge, with the far side 200 metres away through thin air.

Beck peered over the edge, not getting too close. White water raged its way between sharp rocky walls, far below. He remembered the gorge he had seen from the helicopter. This must be the same river.

"Do you know which river it is?" he murmured to Ju-Long. She shook her head.

"This whole region is mountainous, with many rivers flowing into other rivers. Eventually they all become the Xi, which flows into the Pearl River. But this particular one? No."

"Perfect!" Mr Muller said happily. "This takes us exactly where we want to go."

The strip of level ground that was the animal track was now wider, but not much – no more than two or three metres with a cliff on one side and a drop straight down to the river on the other. Beck stared at it, aghast. Was Mr Muller really going to take them along that?

CHAPTER 6

"**W**e are right on course!" Mr Muller announced. "Another hour in this direction will bring us to the caves where we shelter, and from there it will be less than two hours to the planned trail. Look – the track widens further ahead. We will stay there for a five minute break before we push on for the final stretch." He paused. "Just a quick break. We will eat our lunch at the caves when we get there."

A small cheer went up at the mention of lunch. It was close on noon. Breakfast had been some hours ago, and they had all had to work a lot harder than they thought they would since then.

But, *right on course*? Beck thought. Not necessarily. They were right where the GPS said they should be, but that wasn't the same thing. They had no idea what was up ahead. Twenty inexperienced kids making their way on an unplanned route through the jungle, on a ridge two metres wide? This wasn't smart. Problem was, would Mr Muller listen to him if he tried to explain?

Mr Zhou came back to check on the rear of the column.

"It will be a good place to rest," he said. "Eight, nine metres across. Just not a place to spend the night!"

Beck saw his chance. If Mr Muller wouldn't listen, Mr Zhou might.

"Mr Zhou, sir..." Beck began. Mr Zhou held up a hand.

"I know, Beck, I know. Unfortunately, if I disagree with him in public, it might split the group and that would be even worse. We will talk to him when we have stopped."

Beck pictured it in his head: the group splitting in two, each following a different leader. And all the clueless ones would go with Mr Muller. It would be asking for catastrophe. If they stuck together, at least they could help each other out.

And Mr Zhou was going to have a word. With a slightly lighter heart, Beck kept going.

A bit further on, a small stream tumbled down the cliff on their left and cut across the path, before spraying out into the gorge. It must have been an old watercourse – it had cut a small trench half a metre deep and wide. Everyone was able to step over it, one at a time, with care. Beck looked sideways up at the high ground. A lot of rain had fallen up there and it would all be doing what liquid does best – heading downwards, over this ridge. Maybe they needed to take a break up ahead, as Mr Muller planned, but they shouldn't linger.

The track widened into a natural bowl, as Mr Zhou had described. Part of the cliff at the back had eroded away so the ledge extended further away from the drop on their right. It was better sheltered from the wind and it was away from the cliff edge. The ground was still soaking wet from the recent downpour, but there were enough rocks to sit on and the trekkers had enough waterproofs to be comfortable with a brief rest. Many of the expedition swung their backpacks off and dived in for their water bottles and energy snacks.

Mr Muller was busy talking to some of the trekkers. Mr Zhou looked at Beck, and pointed with his eyes at the other leader.

"We will give it a few minutes, Beck, then we will approach him together."

Beck nodded gratefully. He took his pack off but didn't sit down. He preferred standing, letting his muscles relax but also keeping them going. He went to stand as close as was safe to the edge of the cliff and gazed out over across the gorge.

"What is bothering you and Mr Zhou, Beck?" Ju-Long made him jump. He hadn't heard her come up behind him, and he hadn't realised he was showing his feelings so clearly. He gestured with his hand, making short, angry chops in the air.

"Has Mr Muller been along this ledge any further? I doubt it. He didn't know we'd be landing here. How does he know it doesn't just disappear into thin air?"

The new-found confidence he had given her earlier seemed to waver.

"He is following his GPS, Beck."

"Yeah, but one thing a GPS doesn't do is tell you what's round the corner." There were still a couple of minutes left. "I'm going to check. Want to come?"

"Yes, I suppose that would be a good idea."

Beck took a moment to let Mr Zhou know where they were going. An expedition could not have members just vanishing.

"Just take a look," Mr Zhou said after a thought. "Be back in five minutes, then we will have our talk." Beck nodded and picked his pack up again. Out of instinct, he didn't like to be separated from it. He and Ju-Long set off.

Two minutes later, they were out of sight of the others. The ridge curved around an outcropping of rock. Two and a half minutes later, Beck saw that his fears had been proved right. The ridge grew narrower and narrower, and then it simply disappeared into the rock.

On their left was a sheer climb up. On their right, the gorge was no longer quite so sheer. It sloped out again, enough for trees and bushes to take root, and the animal track dived down it. It would be possible for humans to follow but it would still be highly dangerous. They might come to another sheer drop further down, hidden by vegetation, and then people could be killed.

Beck and Ju-Long looked at each other.

"We won't need Mr Zhou's help now," Ju-Long commented. Beck pulled a face.

"As long as Mr Muller believes us. Believes *me*. Come on, let's go and tell him the good news."

They turned and trudged back the way they had come. The camp had just come in sight again around the bend, when Beck heard something.

It was like a sigh, a groan, a whisper on the wind. He and Ju-Long stopped at the same time and looked at each other in puzzlement. It wasn't a sound you heard normally out here, but Beck could tell it was natural. It wasn't made by humans.

And then he *felt* it. A quiver beneath his boots. A shake in the ground, growing stronger. Pebbles began to trickle down the cliff face beside him...

"It's a landslide! Come on!"

He grabbed Ju-Long's hand and they pelted for the camp. It seemed the safest place to be – the wide patch of ground would be more secure than the narrow ridge.

But then a whole chunk of the ridge in front of them simply disappeared, dropping down into the gorge. Ju-Long and Beck just managed to skid to a halt. Beck found himself bent over the new drop, arms waving as he fought to keep his balance and not go over before Ju-Long grabbed onto his pack and hauled him back, away from the edge.

To screams from the trekkers, Beck watched, aghast, as further chunks of the ridge fell away. It was like an invisible giant was taking bites out of the cliff face, chomping his way up to the wide patch of ground where the boys and girls cowered.

On the other side of the camp, the whole cliff face was collapsing. The ridge they had come along was gone. Screaming trekkers trembled as chunks of earth and rubble tumbled down into the camp itself, trying to get away from the danger from above but not too close to the danger in front of them.

One boy in particular stood close to them, petrified, not moving back from the advancing edge. Mr Muller and Mr Zhou and all his friends were shouting at him to move, and he was in tears, but he just didn't seem able to make his legs work. Finally, just as the ground was about to disappear beneath him, Mr Muller ran forward. He grabbed the boy beneath the arms and physically lifted him from the ground, spinning round and hurling him at Mr Zhou.

And then the whole section of cliff and ridge where Mr Muller stood collapsed, above and below, disintegrating into a thousand tons of rubble that plummeted down into the gorge. The air filled with swirling dust and hid the camp from sight.

CHAPTER 7

Beck moved forward as far as he dared, heart pounding, dreading what he might see.

"No, please, no, please..." he whispered, over and over again. He could see nothing through the dust, and even worse, he could hear nothing. He pictured the entire camp, lying buried by rubble at the foot of the cliff. An absolute, total disaster.

But the silence had only been caused by shock and surprise. The gush of relief as shouts and cries came through the dust felt like it could lift him off his feet. They meant people were alive. The dust slowly cleared, and there was the camp. The ground it stood on had got a lot smaller, but it was there.

A dazed Mr Zhou was picking himself up. He and Beck looked at each other across an impassable gulf. It was only a few metres, but it was too far to jump, they had no rope, and they were not going to try and climb along the crumbling, vertical cliff in between.

"Beck –"

"Mr Zhou –"

They both called across at the same time and stopped.

"We're both fine, Mr Zhou," Beck said. "How is everyone else?"

It took Mr Zhou a minute to get the facts. Ju-Long and Beck waited. It wasn't like they had anywhere else to go. Eventually Mr Zhou limped back. It looked like a falling piece of rock had got him on the leg.

"We have cuts and bruises, possibly a broken bone," he reported. "Everyone is alive, apart from –" He stopped abruptly, and looked down at the ground. Beck closed his eyes and groaned as he pictured Mr Muller lying down there at the bottom of the gorge, dead, body crushed and buried by half a cliff.

He could not make himself feel angry with the dead man. There was no sense in dwelling on what had happened. Mr Muller might have been foolish in bringing them here, but he had bravely saved the life of that boy, at the cost of his own. And no one deserved to die in such a way.

When he opened his eyes again he saw that Ju-Long, face white and eyes wide, was staring down at the bottom of the gorge. She was probably picturing Mr Muller the same way he had been. It was not something he was proud of getting used to, but he had seen dead people; he had even seen people die. She very probably had not. He put a gentle hand on her shoulder.

"Concentrate on the living," he said quietly. "We can mourn the dead at any time. The living need us now."

He used as gentle a tone as he could find, because he knew it was harsh advice, but it was also true and it had helped him many times before. She bit her lip and nodded mutely.

"Also," Mr Zhou said, "Mr Muller had the radio on him. We have no way of contacting help."

"Phones?" Beck said, with no sense of hope. The question still had to be asked. Mr Zhou shook his head.

"No signal out here. Too far from home."

Ju-Long started to speak in Standard Chinese, then stopped and started again in English for Beck's benefit. Her voice shook at first but it grew steadier as she faced up to doing what Beck had advised: sticking with the living.

"Mr Zhou, the ridge on both sides of you is gone. Can you climb up the cliff?"

Mr Zhou shook his head again.

"But we still need to get down there. It is … *very* steep."

"It's a lot easier to go down than up," Beck pointed out. "And it won't matter if we bring the cliff down because we'll be going down with it." *As long as it doesn't come down faster than us …* he thought. He didn't say that out loud. If it happened then they would just have to get out of the way. The fact was, the only way was down. "Sure, it's a one-way journey. We won't be coming back up. But we can get ourselves down okay."

"You think so?"

"I'm sure of it," he answered, with a lot more confidence than he felt. It would be hairy, getting down that steep, slippery surface, staying one step ahead of gravity. But it could be done.

She looked unhappily at the edge of the ridge, but then he saw her shoulders square up with resolve.

"Then, we go down," she said.

CHAPTER 8

Recently, in Nepal, Beck had abseiled with ropes down a Himalayan cliff with nothing but hundreds of metres of thin air beneath him.

He had felt safer then than he did now.

Instead of solid rock he only had soft, wet earth to take his weight as he lowered himself backward down the slope. Instead of modern professional-quality nylon rope, he was clinging onto a vine for support.

He could feel it quivering beneath his fingers. It wasn't taking his whole weight – his feet were planted on the cliff – and it was thicker than his finger, so it was tougher than the one that had tripped up the girl earlier, but he wouldn't want to dangle over a precipice holding onto it. Which he just might have to do, if the cliff decided to crumble some more.

The vine was the one that Ju-Long had inadvertently pulled down. He had tied it round the base of a tree near the top of the slope, with a bowline knot. It would get him maybe ten metres in the direction he wanted to go. It wasn't nearly long enough, or strong enough, to get him all the way to the bottom, but it was a start.

He deliberately dug his boots into the soil, challenging it to hold him up. There was no point doing this if they were both going to plunge to their deaths anyway. The vine was insurance. If he decided, within the first ten metres, that this wasn't going to work then he could pull himself back up and they would try to think of another way. Even though Beck was pretty sure there wasn't one.

"It's... okay... I think..." he called, not looking up. Bushes and the bases of trees rooted in the steep slope slowly moved past his face. The ground was covered in a thin layer of dead, mulching leaves, and vines, and roots. Not a lot to get a grip on if he needed to.

"You are coming to the end," Ju-Long called down from above. "Move a little to your right. There is a tree there – you might be able to rest..."

Beck angled himself a little across the slope and felt his boots touch something solid. A tree trunk half as thick as his body grew up out of the soil at a steep angle. The trunk and the slope created a nice notch where he could wedge himself in. The tree seemed able to take his weight, though he had to remember its roots wouldn't be deep. They would be embedded in shallow, damp soil that was all too ready to crumble.

So, he shouldn't linger. He looked further down the slope. It seemed to him that it got shallower, a few metres further down. Once they were down there, it would be less inclined to throw them off.

He let go of the vine and rested his hands on the soil in front of him. It was wet and slippery but he could dig his fingers into it.

"I'm going to move out," he said.

"Beck, be careful –" she protested, but he was already moving. There was no point in delaying.

There was one principle for climbing that always worked exactly the same, in Nepal or here or anywhere. The human body has four points of contact – two hands, two feet. You move one, and one only, at a time. The other three stay anchored. And you only shift your body's weight when all four are steady again – when you've taken a new grip with your hand, or jammed your boot into a fresh foothold.

And so, Beck crabbed sideways and downwards away from the tree and the vine, pressed flat against the slope, arms and legs spread out like a starfish. They had to be like that, because if he brought them closer to his body then the simple act of bending his knees or elbows threatened to push him away. The ground seemed reluctantly willing to hold him as long as he was only passing through. If he slowed down, or stopped, then he felt it begin to give.

But then he felt the unmistakeable pressure against the soles of his feet and he knew he hadn't been imagining it. He breathed out in relief. The cliff really was shallower here. He could even afford to turn around and face outwards, which was his preferred position for going down a slope. If he had tried it earlier, his backpack would have pushed him off. Now he could see where he was going.

"Come down," he called. "It's okay."

But *if it isn't*, he thought, *then we're both dead...*

He kept an eye on her from below as she made her way down the vine. Then, like him, she made the irrevocable decision to let go, and climb down to where he was. He couldn't see her face, but the tension in her frame was obvious. Her climbing badges really had not prepared her for this.

No, he corrected himself: that wasn't fair. She had never climbed with such basic equipment as a vine, but she had the head for heights, and the experience to go with it. Like him, she could put her knowledge to use in situations that it hadn't been expecting.

Her smile as she turned around was drawn. They sat side by side, legs stretched full length below them to hold them up.

Ahead of them was a thin layer of trees, still enough to block out the view across the gorge and to hide what lay below them. Beck only had his memory of seeing the gorge from above to help him guess how far they might still have to go. What with the vine

CHAPTER 13

"**A***agh!*"

His inadvertent shout was jolted out of him when his body hit the rock face. He instinctively clamped his thighs and knees together around the vine for purchase. He bumped again into the rock, sideways on.

He heard the dislodged rock hit the ground below. It was only about the size of a football but it made a smashing, shattering sound that reminded him too clearly of what his own bones would sound like if he fell. In Nepal, he had heard the noise a human body makes when it falls from a great height onto solid stone. He had no intention of being the cause of that sound.

"Beck! Are you all right?"

He didn't answer. He could feel the vine sliding through his legs, even though he was squeezing them together to hold onto it. He locked his elbows hard against his body, though they blazed with the effort, and gripped even more tightly with his hands. He had to force his knees to relax what little grip they had on the vine so that he could stretch a leg out and try to get a foothold on the rock again. On the first try, the tip of his boot merely scraped the surface and almost pushed him away again. The second time, he managed to get his boot into a crack in the rock. That made him steady so that he could get his other foot in as well. He was back to where he had been before the rock fell.

He started up the rock face again, step by step. As he cleared the top, Ju-Long was standing there, hand outstretched to help him.

"It's okay," he grunted. "Don't get too close in case it –"

The edge of the rock crumbled under his foot at precisely that moment. His leg shot away from under him and he fell hard on his front. Every part of him from the waist down was over the drop and he felt gravity drawing on him, pulling him back. The one hand he still had on the vine couldn't get a grip and he felt it sliding through his hand. He scrabbled with the other hand to get a purchase, but his weight held the vine too tight against the ground, and he couldn't get his fingers around it and in half a second the rest of him would be over the edge –

Ju-Long had hold of him. She lay on her front, one hand holding onto the vine to support herself, the other clasping his free hand in a grip like steel. Her arm was bent slightly, with her elbow driven into the ground. He stopped moving and they stared at each other. Beck was the only one of them breathing heavily.

"Climb," she said.

"It's okay," he said shakily. "I don't want to pull you over too –"

"You will not. Just climb."

And so he climbed, using her hand as a purchase. Her arm was so solid it could have been an iron spike driven into the ground to hold him.

A few moments later he was crawling onto solid land. He slowly pushed himself to his feet next to Ju-Long, at the side of the shallow stream that flowed over the edge to become the waterfall.

"*Gaah!*" He flexed his arms and rotated his shoulders to ease the wrenched muscles. "*Whoo!* I am so looking forward to not doing much of that again." He turned to look at her. "How did you do that?"

"Do what?" she asked innocently.

"Hold me!"

"I did not want to let you go, so I did not."

"But –" Perhaps his mind was still jangled from the almost-fall – he struggled to find the words. He was bigger and heavier than her. She should not have been able to hold him like that.

She smiled.

"Not all the body's strength is in the muscles. We all have *ki* within us."

"What's *ki*?"

"It is hard to describe. It is…the energy of the body. Your strength, and your will, combined. I can simply tell my elbow not to bend. It all comes with practice."

"Then I definitely need to practice," he said sincerely. Almost everything Beck knew about survival, he had learned from an expert. He loved to learn new things.

Maybe, he thought, just maybe, it was time for him to stop thinking of all the things Ju-Long had no experience in, and look at the things she *did* know and which he didn't.

"Perhaps I will teach you," she said thoughtfully, "when we have time to stop. Shall we move?"

Beck was forced to push the matter to the back of his mind. Their mission took priority.

He looked ahead. They were at the top of a rocky ledge twenty metres above the river. The good news was, there was no immediate sign of any other vertical rock walls blocking their way. The bad news was, up here the jungle came all the way to the edge. They were back in the same kind of dense undergrowth they had trekked through when the helicopter landed. The air between the trees was damp and laced with the smell of leaves, fresh and rotting. If they had been able to keep to the river shore, they could have made their way from rock to rock with no difficulty – but without food, their energy would have soon failed them. Now, back among the trees, a whole new set of rules applied and the going would be a lot harder – but with that came opportunity.

CHAPTER 14

Beck topped up their bottles up from the stream that plunged over the edge. When he looked up, Ju-Long was holding out a stick for him. She carried another of her own.

"You said earlier you need these for the jungle."

"Absolutely right. Thank you." He took it and gave a couple of experimental thwacks into the palm of his hand. It was good and solid.

"Why do you look so thoughtful?" Ju-Long asked. "We are back in the jungle. You know how to survive in the jungle."

Beck hadn't realised his feelings were showing on his face.

"Just thinking," he said. He adjusted his pack on his shoulders and they set off, angling their route away from the edge of the river. It would be too easy to come to a place at the top of the cliff where the ground had fallen away, disguised by vegetation that couldn't take their weight.

"It would just have been easier and quicker if we could have stuck to the river," he said. "Navigating would be easy because we could have walked along the bank. Food could just come out of the river and we wouldn't have to worry about anything hiding behind trees that wants to eat us. If you want to survive then you make life as easy for yourself as you can. We're only up here because we have to be."

Ju-Long held her arms out.

"But there must be food everywhere! There are more plants and wildlife per square metre in the jungle than anywhere else in the world."

"Oh, absolutely," he agreed, "and all those animals and birds don't live on air, so what they eat, we should be able to eat too. Though if you don't absolutely know which plants are safe, you have to test them and that takes a long time. So we probably won't be eating much vegetarian."

"Why do you have to stop moving to test a plant?" she asked.

"Because it can take a day and a half to do it properly. If you keep moving then by the time you know it's safe, you're a day and a half away from where you found it. And you can't eat anything else in the meantime, because then if you got ill, you wouldn't know if it was the thing you're testing or the other thing." He paused to let her think it through logically. "But, you can't walk through the jungle and not eat anything for thirty six hours – in fact, if you're in a survival situation then you probably shouldn't be moving at all. Nine times out of ten, the best thing to do is stay put and wait for rescue. If Mr Zhou and the others were stranded somewhere safe then the best thing for us to do would be to wait for rescue with them. We're only doing this because they might not have that amount of time to wait."

Just saying that made them remember the little party trapped on the ledge, and they both unconsciously stepped up their pace a little.

"So, what is it that takes all this time?" she asked. He moved a hanging branch away from his face before answering, as he assembled all the facts in his head.

"Okay. The first thing you do is smell it. If it's bitter, throw it away. Same if it smells of peaches – that could mean it's got cyanide in it. If it smells of peaches, throw it away."

"Unless it's a peach."

"Unless it's a peach," he agreed with a chuckle. "Then you use the touch test. You crush some of it and smear it on the back of your wrist, where the skin is soft. If it's really bad then you could get a rash there within a couple of minutes – which is why you also always make sure you've got water available to wash it away with. If you don't get a rash then you put a dab on the inside of your lips or your gums. Give it five minutes to see if they start to tingle, or if any sores develop."

He paused.

"*Then*, you actually chew some, just a tiny bit – but you only swallow the liquid, not the rest of it. This is the really nerve wracking bit, because even if it isn't the kind of poison that blisters your skin, it can still be seriously nasty once it's inside you. And this is where it starts taking time. You need to wait eight hours, and not eat or drink anything else in the meantime."

"That is still only eight hours, and about ten minutes."

"But *then*, if you're still okay, you do the same with a larger amount of food, and you wait five hours."

"Thirteen hours so far..."

"*Then* you eat a whole handful and wait twenty four hours."

"And then?"

"And then tuck in, because it's fine to eat."

He could see Ju-Long was seeing the jungle in a new light. Then, suddenly, he forgot about food and laughed at what he saw ahead.

"Oh, yes! I should have known we'd find this." He hurried forward. Ju-Long came up behind him and gazed with frank bafflement at their discovery.

"Bamboo?" she said. "What is special about that?"

The bamboo grew in a small grove, a few metres from end to end. Vertical, green-grey stalks grew straight up out of the ground, two or three metres high. Some were thicker than his arm, some were the width of a finger, and the others were everything in between. Bamboo always looked to Beck as if it had been assembled rather than grown. It grew in regular sections as if someone had stuck a load of smaller pieces together, each ten or twenty centimetres long, end to end.

"You're not saying we should eat it?" Ju-Long added.

"No, no." Beck reached up to finger the long, thin leaves. "You can eat the shoots, but only if they're well boiled. Eat it raw and it would just clog us up inside. It's almost pure cellulose."

Something tickled against his wrist and he instinctively reached down to scratch it.

"But it'll come in handy for a load of other things... *aah-aah-ahh!*"

Pain shot up his arm as something like a red hot needle jammed itself into the skin of his wrist.

CHAPTER 15

"**A** *ah!*"

Beck bit his lip to shut himself up, and held his wrist up to examine it. A dark red pimple had appeared just below his hand and he could spot the culprit immediately, scuttling away, antenna probing in front of it.

"You little ... thing, you."

"What is it?" Ju-Long hurried up and peered closely.

"Weaver ant."

The ant had reached his wrist and now crawled up onto the palm of his hand. It was a pale brownish-orange, with a long, thin body, only about a centimetre long. It had a bulbous abdomen at the far end which was bigger than the head.

He carefully aimed away from Ju-Long, reached up with his other hand and flicked the little creature away.

"Be careful," she told him. "They are very, very painful."

"You know, I think I just remembered that. They spray formic acid into their bites. Kind of unsporting, if you ask me."

One of the villagers in Borneo had deliberately made an ant bite Beck on the basis that a practical lesson was so much better than theory. Beck had only been little and his screams had made his parents come running, convinced he was being murdered.

This time, he only had himself to blame, he thought wryly. That tickle on his skin had been the ant. It must have dropped onto him off the bamboo. He shouldn't have touched the bamboo without looking more closely, and he certainly shouldn't have scratched that itch without checking what was causing it.

"So, where did it come from?" he wondered out loud. He peered at the bamboo again, from a safe distance. There was a stream of the creatures running up and down the stalk. Taking care not to get too close, Beck began to follow the stream of ants back to its source.

"My grandparents own an orchard," Ju-Long said. "They use ants like these to keep the fruit clear of other insects."

"Well, everything has its uses."

Beck had found it. The ants were trooping in and out of something that looked like a small football, made of leaves that had been sewn together with thin threads of silk. This was how weaver ants got their names. Most ants lived in holes in the ground or in trees. Weaver ants pulled leaves together and sewed them into a nest. It was another habit that made them so useful to the farmers. You could just scoop up a nest, put in a bag, carry it to where you wanted the ants to be, and tip the nest out. Always taking care not to get bitten by a nestful of angry, acid-spitting ants who might not appreciate being relocated.

Beck pulled his knife out and cut himself a thirty centimetre length of bamboo off one of the thinner stalks, first checking it very carefully for any other scuttling, acid-spraying biters. He whittled the end into a fine point with a few firm strokes of the blade and surveyed the nest for a gap between the leaves that made its outer layer. Then, still standing well away from it, he inserted the bamboo into the hole as far as it would go. He kept a careful eye out for angry weaver warriors running up the stick towards him. Most ant nests had guards with the job of protecting the nest from attack, and attacking was definitely what he was doing.

When he withdrew the bamboo, it was covered with what looked like rice grains – and a few ants, despite his precautions.

He flicked them off with the blade of the knife and stepped well away, holding the stick out to Ju-Long.

"Try some larvae," he offered. The 'rice grains' were the stage of ant between egg and full-grown insect. "They bite my hand, I eat their babies. Fair's fair."

He took a pinch between his own fingers and dropped them into his mouth. They burst when he pressed his tongue against the roof of his mouth and released little gusts of spiciness. She looked doubtful, but she also took a pinch.

"They have more protein than beef, pound for pound," he added. "And ants have so many they're not going to miss a few."

After the first nibble, she took another and tucked in with some enthusiasm. Between them they finished off the larvae stuck on the bamboo.

"Perhaps it is better than the same amount of beef, but you would need to eat a lot of it to feel the benefit," Ju-Long pointed out.

"Yeah, and put getting stung to death into the bargain. Still, every little helps. But we'll leave these guys to get on with weaving."

They marched away from the bamboo grove and into the forest.

The cliff loomed large on their right through the trees. The lower slopes were covered in vines and bushes, but there were dark patches too that the vegetation didn't cover. Beck trod closer to have a look and found himself staring into the mouth of a cave. It was as wide as his outstretched arms and a bit taller than a man. Only the rocks at the mouth were visible. It went back further than he could see and the light was swallowed up in the ground.

He hung back. Looking into a cave was like looking into a dark room while you stayed in the light – whoever was in there could see you more clearly than you could see them. And caves in wild places had a tendency to be occupied. They offered shelter and protection and there was usually someone or something who had found that out before you did.

"This part of the country has the largest number of unexplored cave systems in the world," Ju-Long said with a certain amount of pride. "American airmen were sheltered in them during the Second World War."

"That so?" Beck went closer to the cave entrance, stick held at the ready in case anything came charging out. He drew in some short, sharp breaths through his nose. He blew out again just as sharply, only holding the air long enough to get a whiff of it without bringing it into his lungs. Whatever else might be living in there, there was one kind of animal that was a dead cert.

As he had suspected, there was the smell of damp and rot, and a very strong hint of ammonia. Something – a lot of somethings –used this place as a loo. The floor of the cave would be thick with guano, a rich mix of pee and poo. Nothing else seemed to be moving in there.

He checked his watch again. It was four o'clock, drawing on to late afternoon – they had about three more hours of daylight left. Before long they would need food and shelter. The caves would be too unhealthy for shelter – all that guano and the stuff in it would not go well with human lungs – but they could do something about the other thing.

He ran the calculation in his head. Would stopping now to catch food be the best thing to do? Or should they just press on? But if they did that, they might not get another opportunity like this.

He made the decision.

"Well, we need to eat, we've used up those energy bars, and I know what else lives in caves. Apart from American airmen."

"There are, bats, I suppose..." Ju-Long looked at him, wide-eyed. "You want us to eat bats?"

Beck shrugged, with a grin.

"They're mammals. They're protein."

He had absolutely no doubt there was a colony in there, hanging from the ceiling during the day, flying out to hunt small insects at night.

She snorted.

"Good luck if you can catch them. Have you ever seen a bat flying about? They are very small, very fast, and they can detect you before you see them."

"Who said anything about catching them?" he asked. She looked at him uncertainly and he added, "How good are you at tennis?"

CHAPTER 16

"**Y**ou know the really clever thing about bats?" Beck asked conversationally.

He had looked around until he found what he wanted – a tree with branches no thicker than his wrist, growing off in different directions to make a Y. Now he was busy cutting the branch away, using his knife's serrated blade.

"They are almost blind, and fly at night using sonar?" Ju-Long suggested over her shoulder. He had asked her to gather up a good length of vine. It had to be thin – much thinner than the one they had used to get up the cliff. It couldn't be much thicker than a finger, if that. She had found a good cluster of it and was busy pulling it out of the bush where it was entwined with the plant's own leaves and branches.

"Well there's that," Beck agreed. He kept sawing – the branch was almost free. "But the *really* clever thing is – their wings are basically skin stretched between very long fingers. They fly by extending their fingers out as far as they will go and waving them up and down..."

The branch had come free. Beck squatted down and quickly lopped off the ends of the two smaller branches, and the leaves and twigs that grew from it. Now he had a Y-shaped piece of wood the size of a tennis racket.

"What is your point?"

Beck grinned and held up both his own hands, fingers out, and waggled them.

"So they are the only animal in the world that flies by the power of jazz hands!"

First, she looked puzzled. Then she rolled her eyes. Then she turned back to the vine and he saw her shoulders starting to quiver.

"That... that is... so bad it is... almost good," she said between giggles.

"Almost," Beck agreed with a smile. He finished trimming down his branch. "How's the vine?"

"I have about two metres of it."

"Perfect." Beck described what she needed to do next. She didn't look convinced.

"That will work? Have you seen it done?"

"I've heard of it," Beck admitted. "Not seen it. But it's a trick used by the Li tribe of southern China, so... well, we're in southern China, aren't we?"

And so, Ju-Long got busy as he had asked. She started to lace the vine between the two arms of the Y-branch, from side to side and up and down until it made a loose net. It made the piece of wood look like a very crude tennis racket.

To catch the bats, Beck needed two things – the Y-branch racket, and a flaming torch. While Ju-Long was busy with the first item, he cut off a length of bamboo, about half a metre long. He gripped the bamboo between his knees, placed the sharp edge of his knife's blade across the top of the branch, and started to saw, carving out a notch down the rim of the tube simultaneously on opposite sides. When he had gone down about twenty centimetres he pulled the blade out, then rotated the bamboo branch a little and started again.

Another great feature of bamboo was that its sections were hollow. By the time he had done this five or six times, the top twenty centimetres of the branch had been reduced to thin strips of bamboo, all joined at one end to the solid part of the piece.

He gave one of the strips a prod with a finger, moving the tip outwards. When he took his finger off it, it snapped back into position.

He needed something to burn in the torch, and so he burrowed down into the undergrowth where Ju-Long had found the vine. Two or three layers down, the dead leaves were bone dry. It was the same in tropical jungles or in woods back home in England – the top surfaces of leaves could be so tightly packed that they waterproofed whatever was beneath them. It could be a real fire hazard, if people were going to walk through a wood smoking, or light a camp fire, thinking everything was too wet to burn. Here he actually wanted it to burn – in a controlled way.

Beck gathered the dry leaves together and stuffed them down between the bamboo strips. The pressure of the leaves pushed the strips outward, and the strips' own springiness held them in place.

Meanwhile, Ju-Long had finished her task. She took a grip on the Y-branch in both hands and hefted it about, experimenting with a couple of lunges as though she were knocking an invisible ball out of the air. The vines stayed firm.

"I think this will hold."

"Great. Could you hold this, please?"

Ju-Long held the torch while Beck pulled the fire steel out from around his neck. She looked sceptically at the two pieces of metal.

"That will set light to these?"

"Watch and learn!" He struck the flat scraper against the small rod, and she recoiled as sparks sprayed through the air and into the leaves. Immediately he leaned down and blew gently onto them – not hard enough to blow them out, but enough to give them the steady flow of oxygen they needed.

A couple of spots on top of the leaves started to turn black and spread. Holes appeared in the leaves, growing rapidly larger while their edges charred. Thin wisps of smoke started to curl upwards and his nose caught the sharp, sweet smell of natural burning.

The air above the torch began to shimmer with heat, and more and more smoke poured upwards. Within a minute, the end of the torch was burning bright and a thick column of smoke streamed into the air.

"Right," he said with satisfaction. "Let's get us some survival food."

CHAPTER 17

Beck shrugged his coat off, then pulled the front of his sweatshirt up so that it covered his nose and mouth. With one hand he held it in place; with the other he took the torch from Ju-Long. The bat guano that coated the floor of the cave would be a breeding ground for the *Histoplasma capsulatum* fungus. Get that into your lungs and you could quite possibly get stuck with a case of histoplasmosis, starting with breathing difficulties and potentially ending in organ failure. The shirt was to protect his lungs. It was only a crude filter, but it would do.

Ju-Long picked up the Y-branch and together they approached the mouth of the cave. Ju-Long waited a couple of metres outside it, feet apart, branch gripped in both hands.

Beck went on, deeper into the cave. The ammonia smell was strong, even through the cloth. It was like sticking needles into his nostrils and he could feel his eyes starting to water. He held the torch at arm's length ahead of him and waved it gently about. Smoke billowed upward and spread across the ceiling. Any moment now...

Something like a black bullet came whizzing towards him out of the darkness. With some effort, he didn't flinch. The bat would be sensing him with ultrasonic signals, and he knew its navigation system would tell it to get out of his way. Sure enough it whirred past him, a few centimetres from his ear. He just had time to glimpse the small, furry body between two rapidly working wings before it was past him.

More dark shapes came flying out at him as the bats started to swarm, spooked by the smoke from the torch. They flowed around his stationary figure and headed for the daylight.

Where Ju-Long waited with the branch.

"*Hi-yah!*"

Ju-Long swiped with the branch at the first bat to fly past. It only just avoided her. She lunged immediately at another, with another shout. She missed that one, too, but now she was getting used to the way they moved. She hit the third one. The net of vines thwacked the creature out of the sky. It hit the ground, stunned, and fluttered briefly before she brought her boot down sharp on its head.

The bats were still swarming so she left it and struck out at the next one to come past her. This one hit the ground and lay still, but she finished it off just in case it was only knocked out.

The bats could avoid anything that was stationery. They were less well equipped to deal with something that moved rapidly, and the net wasn't solid enough for their sonar to fix on.

Ju-Long yelled, "*Hi!*", and swung again, and again. In the end, the fifth bat was the last. The swarm had flown on now, disappearing into the trees to seek out a fresh cave that wasn't full of smoke.

"Wow," Beck said sincerely. The Li tribe's bat-catching trick certainly worked, and it felt appropriate to be watching a Chinese girl doing it. She grinned, breathing a little heavily, like she had just come through a physical workout.

"Did you know that our word for 'bat' translates as 'happiness'?" she asked.

"And are you feeling happy?"

"Oh, yes!"

The torch had almost burned itself out. Beck tipped the smouldering leaves out onto solid rock and trampled them to extinguish the flames for good. He did not want to start a forest fire.

Ju-Long held one of the bats up by its rear leg. The wings hung like leather flaps. The body was like a misshapen mouse, with dark fur, big ears and an ugly, scrunched up face. "Do we eat these now?"

"Not yet. A lot of bats carry rabies –" She held the bat quickly at arm's length, before she remembered it was dead and not going to attack her. "... So we need to cook them well. It's a better use of our time if we do that when we've stopped anyway to camp. Let's go a bit further. I want to see if we can find something else."

"What a shame. I've worked up quite an appetite."

They put the bats into Beck's pack and strode on. Every step was one step closer to getting help for Mr Zhou.

***

The sound of the river was never far away, and as they headed into the trees it seemed stronger than before. Beck could also hear the noise of a waterfall – water gushing over rocks and plunging into a pool.

And then he saw where it came from.

To their right, a waterfall fell straight down the side of the river gorge. The stream of water had cut a ravine through the trees and down to the river, and it went right across their path.

Beck peered cautiously over the edge and looked down at the churning water. It surged white and furious, ten metres below. The far side of the ravine was about five metres away.

"Okay, we're not getting over this in a hurry. Let's see what it's like further on."

They turned left, down towards the river, following the water below them.

They soon found that the ravine opened up straight into the river. There was no slope down to a beach – no way they could easily get down to the level of the water and get across.

They turned around and went as far as they could back up the ravine, right to the point where the waterfall came down. The sides of the gorge were matted with damp vegetation. Beck had hoped they might be able to climb across, but now he could see immediately that the waterfall would just wash them away if they tried. Some waterfalls had empty spaces behind them that climbers could pick their way through, but this one flowed down the rock itself.

"Okay," Beck said through his teeth. "This is really annoying."

The ravine completely blocked their path. There was no way ahead at all.

Time to get creative, he pondered.

CHAPTER 18

Beck's thoughts spun as he stared at the barrier in their way.

The only way across was to climb down, get across the rushing stream, and climb up again. It was not going to be easy. Okay, they could probably use some vines as a climbing rope to get down. But the only way across the stream would be to go through it. He had another look down. It was far too fast for wading across. They would have to find a spot where there were rocks sticking out which they could use as stepping stones. The rocks, if they existed, would be slick and wet. One wrong step and they would be swept away. If they were lucky, they wouldn't be battered to death before they were flushed out into the river.

And if they made it across, then they would have to get up the far side. It was sheer, and he couldn't see any useful hanging vines that they could use to climb up again.

"Do you think this could hold our weight?"

Ju-Long broke into his thoughts. She had been looking at the ravine with just as much dismay as him, but now she was crouched down to examine a fallen log. It was about three metres long and as wide as a telegraph pole.

"Well..." Beck went to join her, and examined it with a critical eye. It looked solid and wasn't rotten. He gave it a kick to test it. "Yeah, probably. But it's too short to get across that gap."

"It does not have to go all the way. Give me a hand and I will show you."

Between them, they carried the log a short distance to where a tree grew out at an angle across the ravine.

"I saw this earlier," Ju-Long said. The tree stretched about halfway over. Further out, it forked into a Y, like a larger version of the branch she had used to bring down the bats. She put one foot on its trunk and pressed down. The tree flexed, but its roots didn't budge. "This will certainly hold us."

"It only gets us half way, though…oh." Beck saw what she had in mind. He looked down at the piece of wood they were carrying. "Right."

Very carefully, because the edges of the ravine were slick with dead, wet leaves, Ju-Long let herself down to sit astride the tree. Beck pushed the log towards her and she took hold of the end, then held it under one arm while she worked her way along the trunk towards the Y-fork. Her legs dangled on either side over thin air and rushing water far below. Beck stood on firm ground and held the other end of the log, feeding it forward as she went, inch by careful inch. He kept one eye on the roots of the tree. If he thought they were going because of her weight, he would shout to her to climb back immediately. There wasn't any amount of ki that would let her levitate.

She came to the fork in the tree, which was as far as she could go, and rested her end of the log in it. Then, slowly, she pushed it forward. Beck could no longer hold onto it and it was entirely in her hands. Bit by bit, the log extended through the fork and over the gushing stream. Eventually more than half its length was sticking out and its weight made it want to tip forward into the ravine. Ju-Long gripped the trunk more firmly with her knees to counter the log's weight and to stop it taking her with it.

Finally, the far end was over ground on the other side of the ravine. She let it drop down with a thud. Her end stayed wedged in the Y-fork. Between them, the tree and the log now made a very slender bridge across the ravine.

"Brilliant!" Beck applauded, though he could already see that staying balanced on the log would be very difficult. Still, the way to solve problems was to take them one at a time. "Now – *woah!*"

He lunged forward to stop her but he couldn't do anything. Ju-Long had leaned forward too far, had lost her balance and toppled into the abyss.

there was a lot of dead wood lying around and they would almost certainly find larvae and grubs beneath the bark.

Just as he was about to suggest they did just that, he heard something else. A distant, faint croak.

"Okay... I think I can get us something to eat right now – if you don't mind French food?"

CHAPTER 20

"That is not French," Ju-Long said, puzzled, a few minutes later. "That is Chinese. We are in China."

"I know – sorry," said Beck. "English joke."

They both looked down at the frog in his hand.

It hadn't been hard to find. Beck's ears had led them to a series of marshy pools at the edge of the gorge. Water trickled down from above, running out of cracks in the rock rather than tumbling down in a full blown waterfall. The pools were still and shallow – a pleasant change from the rampaging water that Beck was getting used to in this place. Clusters of reeds and marsh-grass grew out of the water, and it was in one of these that Beck found the frog.

It was a good size – about the same size as his hand if he spread out all the fingers. He held onto it firmly.

"You are sure it's safe to eat?" Ju-Long asked.

"Positive." He had taken great care to identify it visually before he picked it up. "It's not warty, so it's not a toad." Its grey-green skin was smooth and sleek. "And it's not brightly coloured, which would mean it's poisonous." In South America, Beck had seen frogs so bright that they could have been dipped in luminescent paint. The slime on their backs could cause hallucinations, or paralyse your nervous system. He had met hunters who would use drops of frog slime on their arrows to bring down their prey.

Beck put the point of his knife at the base of the frog's head – where its neck would be, if frogs had necks.

"Sorry," he said quietly to himself, and thrust through the frog's spinal cord. The frog twitched and went still.

Beck quickly sliced the rest of the way across the neck. Its blood was thin and watery. He stuck his finger into the gash and worked it between the frog's skin and its flesh, lubricated by the juices inside its body. The two came apart quite easily, with only a little resistance. Gradually he was able to work the top half of its body out of the hole, then peel back the whole of the skin, down to its thighs and beyond. The guts came with it – a small pile of rubbery tubes full of digestive acid, and half-digested food, and frog poo, all crammed full of bacteria. If they got into contact with the rest of the body, the best case scenario was they would make it taste foul. Much more likely, they would make it inedible, if not poisonous.

"This frog," he said as the skin came away from the frog's hind feet, "is going to give us valuable energy. Energy that we're going to use to save the others."

Without the skin, the frog's body was a pale pink, with about the same amount of flesh as a turkey drumstick.

"Here you go." Beck passed it to Ju-Long, who took it with a kind of horrified fascination. "Perfectly safe to eat raw. You have this one – I'll get another."

It only took him a few more minutes. He had taken the frog out of the pool, so none of its blood had dripped into the water to warn its friends. He soon found another, again following the convenient croaks. Its flesh, when he ate it, was slimy and cold, but it felt good in his stomach, giving his body something solid to call on as he continued to burn those 1000 calories per hour.

"Feeling better?" he asked brightly. Ju-Long gave a queasy smile.

"I think so. I can keep going with that inside me for a few more hours."

"Yeah, well, it won't be that long. We'll stop for the night the next time we come to some bamboo. There must be some more soon."

She frowned.

"What has bamboo to do with it?"

"You'll see!"

He looked at his watch, then glanced up at the sky. The sun was already well past the edge of the gorge, so the land around them was rapidly dimming. The thick typhoon clouds that still boiled above meant it would get dark even quicker. And nothing is quite so pitch black as night in the jungle. No street lights, no towns, no cities to cast the ever-present light of humanity – and very probably no stars or moon either, blocked out by the tree canopy. It would be far too easy to get lost or injure themselves in the pitch dark.

That was, if they didn't get eaten first. At night, snakes and other animals came out on the hunt. Night time in the jungle brought a whole new set of challenges, and it would be on them very soon.

CHAPTER 21

They marched another twenty minutes before they found what Beck was looking for. A grove of bamboo trunks the size of scaffolding poles.

"Perfect!" he said. And as if on cue, it began to rain.

The poles grew up from among a scattered pile of rocks, large and small, which must have fallen down from the edge of the gorge and rolled a short distance to this place. So, Beck reckoned, if all the available rocks had fallen, that meant there wouldn't be any more coming down. That made this a doubly suitable place for a camp.

On top of the rain, a low rumble of thunder drifted down the valley. Beck cocked an eye up at the gorge lip. Up there it would be blowy and wet. Down here it would still be wet, but at least relatively sheltered. He was more concerned with the dwindling light. They would have a gloomy sort of twilight for no more than an hour down here, with the residue of daylight above them. Once the sun had set at the top of the gorge, down here the dark would be impenetrable.

"Do you know how to build a fire?" he asked.

"Of course." Ju-Long sounded a little affronted that he should ask. "It was part of the Young Pioneer course."

"Great." Without hesitating, Beck reached into his shirt and pulled the fire steel over his head. He handed the dangling pieces of metal over to her. "Then please will you? We can cook the bats on it."

And so Ju-Long started to gather up kindling and tinder for a fire, while Beck got to work on the bamboo.

He worked quickly because he was going to have to do this twice, once for each of them. They couldn't spend a night sleeping on the jungle floor. The mulch of dead and rotting vegetation would soak into their bones, chilling them as they slept. And any number of creepy crawlies would want to join them. For warmth and comfort, they had to be off the ground, even if it was only by a few inches.

First Beck selected a thick green bamboo pole, about as thick as a man's forearm, after checking it very carefully for ants. He sawed through its base and then cut the tip off, leaving him with a simple bamboo pole about two metres long.

He cut a notch a short distance from one end, using a stone to hammer the knife blade in. Then he slid the knife down the length of the pole, slicing off a section to reveal its hollow interior. He stopped a short distance from the other end. Now the pole was a hollow tube at either end, but only half a tube in the middle.

Next Beck jammed the knife tip first into the wood of the cut-out section, again starting at one end and working the knife down towards the other. He did this several times, so that now the half-section of the pole consisted of several vertical strips, joined to the rest of the pole at either end.

When Beck stood the pole up on one end and pressed down, the strips splayed out into the shape of a hammock. He now had the basics of where Ju-Long would be spending the night – but only the basics. It returned to its natural pole shape the moment he stopped applying pressure. If Ju-Long lay on it like it was now, the strips would try to close up around her. To prevent that happening, he cut a length of vine and wound it through and around the strips, tying them into place so they stayed in their hammock shape.

He still had to keep it off the ground. He cut another pole, taller than he was, and sawed it into four equal sections. Then he cut some lengths of vine and tied two sections into the shape of a letter X, with one end of the hammock pole secure in the notch where the two pieces crossed. He did the same with the other two sections and the other end of the hammock.

He stepped back to admire his handiwork. Pretty good, though he said so himself. Of course, he would have to do it all over again to make a hammock for himself, but right now he could take a short break.

"How's the fire going?" he asked.

It was a rhetorical question. He could see with his own eyes that it was crackling away nicely, and the light it provided was already invaluable.

Ju-Long had found a couple of flat stones to build it on, and she had assembled the fire's three parts in the shelter of a small rock. Any fire consisted of tinder, kindling and fuel. The tinder was the first stage of getting the fire going, and she had made a pile of small twigs and dry leaves from the bone-dry layers hidden away beneath the ivy. That was what she set fire to with the fire steel. It only needed a few sparks to fall on the leaves. Immediately, like Beck lighting the torch, she had started to blow gently on the singeing leaves. The fire had spread quickly.

The kindling was thin, dead bamboo strips laid across the pile. It had caught fire from the tinder and kept going long enough to burn the fuel that provided most of the heat. While he was making the shelter, Beck had heard the first distinctive *crack* which meant that any moisture trapped inside the kindling was turning to steam and bursting its way out. That was always the moment when you knew the fire had taken hold.

But without fuel, the fire would quickly burn itself out. Ju-Long had dragged larger pieces of wood out from the undergrowth and laid them on top of the pile. They were thick and they took time to start burning, but once they had caught they burnt slowly and steadily. They released their heat bit by bit, rather than all at once. She had put aside a small pile of reserve wood to add to the fire whenever it needed stoking.

Beck took a moment to crouch down and hold his hands out to the warmth while Ju-Long examined the hammock.

"That is a very clever idea. Where did you learn it?"

"I saw it done in that village I mentioned in Borneo. Never actually done it myself until now. Now I just have to do one more for myself."

"I can possibly help a little." She looked around for a suitable branch. "Would this work?" she asked, selecting a stick about as thick as a scaffolding pole.

"Yup, that'll do." He began to pass her his knife. "Do you want to cut –"

In one fluid movement Ju-Long stood up, moved her feet slightly apart, raised her hand and swung it down at the base of the branch.

"*Hi!*"

All the motion and energy of her body and her arm seemed to flow into her hand as it passed through the wood, and the branch tumbled down with a sharp crack.

CHAPTER 22

Beck felt his eyes boggling out of his skull.

"May I just say – *wow?*"

She gave him a shy, sideways smile, and picked the pole up. "Please hold this where you would like it cut...?"

So Beck held the remains of the branch with his hands either side of the two metre mark. He tried not to flinch as her hand flashed in front of his eyes and sliced through the wood, leaving him with a piece in each hand.

"How do you do that?" Then he remembered her little demonstration when she had saved him from falling down the cliff, and he answered his own question. "*Ki*, right?"

"Indeed." She held her hand up in front of her, angled so that he could see the edge and the heel, just above where it joined her wrist. "But, you must make sure that this is the part that hits the wood. I can't make my body stronger than it is – I could not use flesh and bone to cut through metal. But this part of you can take a lot of force, provided it is the part that makes contact. Your *ki* will drive it through."

"Doesn't it hurt?"

"What would it feel like if you hit your hand very hard against a wall?"

"It would hurt!"

"Exactly! So that is the answer to your question. Pain is your body taking precautions because it fears you will damage it.

Provided you know what you are doing, your body is not always right."

It's only pain... That had been what Beck's Scout instructors used to say as they urged twenty panting, sweating, exhausted boys over assault courses or on cross country runs, lungs burning and with legs that felt like jelly. It was a motto he had had to repeat to himself many times. Ju-Long wasn't wrong.

"You learn to push yourself beyond your self-imposed limitations," she said. "Those include fear and pain and self-doubt. You must imagine your hand going through the wood. If you can't see it inside your head, it will not happen outside."

"Be at one with the chop," Beck said wryly.

"That is precisely it!" She sighed. "I would try to teach you, but... I have done this for so long I cannot remember beginning to learn. I doubt you would make much of a pupil in the short time available. No offence."

"None taken," Beck assured her. An idea occurred to him. He looked up to check the sky, then out into the jungle, where it would soon be too dark to see anything at all, even with the firelight. "Do you think you could finish the second hammock off?" She nodded and he passed her the knife.

"And what will you be doing?" she asked as she set to work.

"Me? I need to place our breakfast order with room service..."

CHAPTER 23

Getting the skin off the bats was more fiddly than it had been with the frog. Beck cut off their heads and wings, then had to slice gently with the tip of the knife, from the neck and down the stomach to between the hind legs, taking great care not to pierce the guts en route. Like most mammals, the bats had a layer of fat between their skin and their flesh, which glued them together. He had to use the knife to cut through the strands of fat and pull them apart. Then he used a finger to hook the guts out of the bat's body cavity. They plopped out onto the ground with slick little squelches, and lay in small, wobbly piles of tubes that glistened in the firelight.

Beck left the bats on a rock and slid the slimy mess of guts into a coat pocket. He paced a short distance away from the camp and crouched down to look closely at the undergrowth, turning his head slowly until he could see what he was after. It was important not to look back at the fire, as that just erased his night vision. But with his back to the flames and his eyes taking in their light reflected back from the bushes around him, he could see what he needed to. The undergrowth grew tightly together, but in places you could see where some small animal had pushed its way through.

And where one animal did that, another would follow, and another, and another. They would always take the easiest route rather than push their own way through.

Now he needed a rock, and there were plenty of fallen rocks to choose from, scattered around and among the bamboo. He chose one which was flat and heavy enough to need both hands to lift, but not so heavy that it would just crush anything. He dusted the dead leaves off it and lugged it back to the tunnel.

Next he looked around for a reasonably sturdy stick – one that was strong enough to hold one end of the rock up without breaking. He put the rock down next to the tunnel, lifted up one end and jammed the stick under it.

The stick promptly snapped and the rock fell down. Beck rolled his eyes. Okay, try again. He needed patience for this job – that was always a useful survival habit.

The next stick was too long for what he had in mind, so he snapped it over his knee. He wedged one of the halves between ground and rock, and this time it worked – the stick held the end of the rock off the ground, over the path that the animal would take into its leaf tunnel.

And it would serve no purpose at all, because an animal could just trot under it without knocking the stick. It needed one final touch. He lifted the rock off, took up a length of bat intestine and skewered it onto the end of the stick. Then he gently set the rock back where it had been. Any hungry critter during the night that took a nibble would try to pull the intestine away, which would pull the stick down – and that would be the last thing the animal knew.

Beck set up four more traps like the first, in different places – two also using a rock, the other two using heavy logs. The more traps he set, the greater his chances of catching something – there was no guarantee any trap on its own would be successful. Not if the animals had decided to take a different route that night. But if you don't try, you don't succeed. Beck knew that applied to everything in survival.

By then, the bat guts were all used, the light was almost gone, and rain was coming. He could smell it on the wind; it blew warmer on his face, he could hear the rushing in the trees, and the smells of the jungle seemed to grow richer in preparation. He made his way back to the camp, guided by the orange glow of the fire.

Ju-Long had finished the second hammock and laid the two of them side by side on the other side of the fire to the rock. The warmth from the fire would reflect off the rock towards them. She had also cut off new, fresh poles for an overhead shelter. Having hammocks to sleep in was all very well, but not if they were open to the sky, when the sky was likely to dump a million gallons of water on them at a moment's notice. She had jammed four of the poles into the ground to make a rectangle around the two hammocks, and used vine to tie longer poles to the tops of the four vertical ones, making a framework of bamboo that surrounded the hammocks.

She had topped it off with palm leaves – nature's guttering, growing with V-shaped leaves that channelled water away from the central stalk. She had gathered several clusters to cover the framework, laid over the horizontal poles and tied into place, making sure that they overlapped. Any rain that missed one leaf would be bound to hit another, and it would all drip away from the sleepers in the shelter below.

They admired the finished product together, and Beck nodded in approval. It wasn't windproof, but it would keep the rain out and that was the key thing. They would be able to sleep, not in a great deal of comfort, but more comfortably than they would on the ground. They would be relatively warm and dry.

There were two more things to do. Beck jammed a pair of bamboo sticks into the ground and peeled his boots off. Ever since he had crawled out of the river that day, he had been walking with his feet in a moist, squelching steam bath, unable to dry out properly. It wasn't just a matter of comfort. If he kept his feet in wet boots for too long then he ran a serious risk of some nasty fungus deciding to breed between his toes. He set the boots upside down, one on each spit, angled so that the warmth from the fire would get into them.

"You too," he instructed Ju-Long. "Then, dinner!"

The fire had burnt itself into a glowing, orange mass of embers. The fuel logs were wrapped in flame and crackling merrily away, and the air above them shimmered with heat.

They sat barefoot on a pair of rocks. Ju-Long had cut a couple of thin bamboo spits from one of the cut-out sections of bamboo. They skewered the first two bats and held them over the fire, turning them slowly. The bats' pale flesh took a while to brown nicely.

"I have no idea how long to cook them for," she said frankly, "but I want to make sure any rabies in them is well and truly dead."

Beck gave the little cooking creature a check.

"It will be," he said. "Any virus is pretty fragile once its host animal is dead. As long as the meat is medium done, we'll be safe."

Ju-Long silently passed him a skewer, with an unspoken message: *go on, then, be the first.* He held the bat up to his mouth. It did not look appetising, but the smell of something cooked so close to his nose reminded the rest of him just how hungry he was.

"I'll be the official taster, then," he said, and he bit into the small body.

CHAPTER 24

The wood smoke had added some flavour to the meat, which was fortunate, because otherwise it tasted exactly like what it was – a creature that had grown up and lived in a damp cave. He pulled a face, but kept eating. He tore off the accessible meat with his teeth, then carefully nibbled and sucked at every bone to get every last scrap off. They hadn't killed these bats for fun – it had been to stay alive. They owed it to the bats to make use of every last bit of them.

Ju-Long tucked hungrily into hers. With the first two bats out of the way, they cooked the last three, eating another one each and sharing the last between them. By the end, even though it had not been the best meal in the world, they had stomachs that were half full of cooked meat, and it felt good. The heat sent strength out into tired limbs and set them up for a good night's sleep.

But even though a good night's sleep was exactly what his body cried out for, there was something else Beck wanted to deal with. She had said she would teach him – *perhaps* she would teach him – when they stopped. They had stopped now. They were quietly sitting and looking into the flames, with no further plans. He took a breath.

"So," he said. "*Ki.*"

She took her time responding, and he began to wonder if he should repeat himself.

"You would like to learn how to do it," she said, not looking away from the fire.

"Uh-huh."

She smiled.

"And how old are you?"

"Fourteen."

"I am nearly that age and I have been practicing all my life. So you could begin to learn now, and by the time you are twenty-eight, we will see how well you are doing."

He laughed.

"Yeah, I know. And I've been doing what I do all my life too. But there's always something new to learn. A little knowledge is better than none." She look at him sideways, doubtfully, and he glanced around for an example. "Look, I've not made hammocks like those before – but I've seen it done and someone once taught me how to cut wood, so I could add those two little bits of knowledge together, and use my experience, and put the hammocks together. Everything starts with little bits of knowledge."

Still she simply looked sideways at him. Suddenly she held up her hand as though she were challenging him to an arm wrestling match. It was her left hand, though he knew she was right handed.

"Take my hand. Try to move it."

He did so, and found that it was as though her arm were made of iron. The muscles of his own arm strained, and he couldn't make hers budge.

"I will now move your arm," she said. "Try to stop me."

He tensed his arm muscles as much as he could.

"O –" he began, but he never got to "...kay." His arm folded so easily it could have been putty. The rest of his body had to bend at the waist to stop her breaking it.

"Would you like to use both hands?" she asked. He paused, then laughed. He knew when he was beaten, even if he couldn't tell how.

"Thanks, but I enjoy having my arms attached to my shoulders."

"I doubt I could pull them out. I do not have superhuman strength. I cannot do the impossible – I could not fly or walk on water or pick up a car, or any of those things you see in movies.

"But you can tell your body what to do," he said, remembering her earlier explanation at the top of the cliff.

"To an extent. What did you feel when you were hanging from that log?"

He thought back.

"I ... I guess I pictured it in my head. To be honest – a lot of it was doing what I've often done anyway."

"Then you are already some way there. Now you have a name for it. You must be calm, unafraid, aware of your body. You already have the instinct. There are exercises, which I can teach you, but you must do them regularly, without fail, every day for many days. I suppose I can lay some groundwork." She turned abruptly to face him. "Close your eyes."

He paused, surprised, but then did so.

"Now, sit so that your body is balanced. Your spine straight, your muscles relaxed ..."

It meant sitting up a little, but he adjusted his posture, seated on his rock. He felt her take his head and tilt it slightly forward.

"You can keep your eyes closed, or keep them part open and look at something unimportant. Hold this position with your muscles relaxed. Place your hands together, fingertips touching, over your stomach." He obeyed. "Ki flows through your body like water through a tunnel. If it is obstructed, it cannot flow. So you must always have the correct posture. Now, breathe. As you did before, in and out. Be aware of every breath in – how it brings oxygen into your lungs, providing energy that spreads and powers the cells of your body. And be aware of every breath out – you are expelling carbon dioxide, a waste gas of use to plants but none to you. So, you are exchanging energies between the world inside and out. Energy is flowing. Do this until I tell you to stop."

Beck didn't know how long it went on. A minute, five minutes, ten. He found it easier with her second option, of keeping his eyes slightly open – otherwise there was a danger he would simply nod off.

"Raise your right hand," she said eventually. Calmly, without fuss, Beck raised it up to shoulder height. He felt Ju-Long's fingers close around his own, as they had before.

"In a moment I will try to move your hand again. This time, do not permit it."

Beck nodded. His mind was so unbothered, so tranquil, it was as if she was telling him the sky was blue. Nothing unusual, nothing alarming.

"I will do it – now."

He felt the pressure of her hand against his suddenly change. But this time, he resisted. It wasn't by tensing his muscles or actively pushing back, though he knew that must be happening. It was at a higher level. He simply did not want his arm to move; that was the command his brain sent his body, and his body could make it happen however it liked.

And his arm stayed where it was, as though it was set in concrete. It wasn't numb, he knew it belonged to him, he could feel everything – and it was staying.

His eyes flew open and he stared at it.

"Wow!"

And that was enough to break the spell and for normal service to be resumed. His arm abruptly folded under the pressure. She let go before she twisted him off his seat.

"That was a good start. And now, I think we should sleep."

She laid herself carefully down on her bamboo hammock and shifted experimentally. It creaked and rocked but it stayed steady as she relaxed into it.

"This really is quite comfortable."

Beck had been holding his hand up, studying it and flexing it. He dragged his attention back to where he was.

"As long as you don't wriggle too much, you'll be fine."

"Hmm." She pulled her hood up to cover her head, and did her coat up as far as it would go. It was the nearest either of them would get to blankets, but it was an important step. They were sheltered from the rain but not the wind, and the human body cools down as it sleeps. Ju-Long was taking care to preserve as much of her warmth as she could. Wrapped up like that, with the fire just an arm's length away, she did look very cosy.

"I –" She paused, looking up at him. "I have not stopped thinking about the others."

"I know. Me too," he said softly. She nodded.

"Time passes more quickly if you sleep." She closed her eyes.

Beck got their bottles and placed them under the end leaves of the shelter's roof. When it rained, water would be channelled down the V-shaped leaves and they would fill up automatically.

Last of all, he tossed some damp leaves on the fire. Smoke started to billow almost at once, and it would keep the mosquitoes away. Then he wrapped himself up in his own hammock, as Ju-Long had done, coat tight around him and hood pulled up over his head. A brilliant flash lit up the sky, and a mighty clap of thunder echoed down the gorge. And then the rain came – first a pattering, then a hiss, then a roar as the skies opened and splattered onto the palm leaf roof.

To a city person, he thought as his eyes grew heavy, this might be terrifying. Loud noises, big flashes, and an overpowering sense of being too small and weak to do anything about it. You were totally at the power of uncontrollable forces that were stronger than you. Some people just longed for the security of four walls and a roof over their heads.

But Beck knew he was surrounded by nature doing what nature did best – looking after itself, replenishing the earth in its own way. He respected nature and did not feel a stranger here. He had done what he could to make Ju-Long and himself comfortable. After that, what happened, happened.

But the one dent in his feeling of comfort – his last thought as he went to sleep, and his first when he woke the next morning – was like hers. Mr Zhou, and the party trapped on that ledge. How would they be doing in this weather?

Just before he fell asleep, Beck made a prayer and a vow, that this would be their last night in the jungle. Tomorrow they would find help. They had to, for the sake of everyone who was relying on them.

CHAPTER 25

Beck woke up, sore and stiff, into a world washed clean by the rain, where every leaf dripped with fresh water. The smells of the jungle were fresh in the damp wind that still gusted past the shelter, and he could hear the river surging with renewed energy in the background.

The clouds at the edge of the typhoon still boiled thick overhead, letting red sunlight through with a reluctant glow. Beck was actually grateful for the overcast day. If the sun had been shining directly onto them, most of the moisture left by the rain would have turned to steam. Down here, with nowhere for that steam to go, it would have been like walking through a sauna.

He checked the time: six a.m. He had slept right through the night, right through the rain, finally letting his body feel tired after the day before.

He grunted as he clambered up out of the hammock. It had kept him relatively warm, and dry, but it wasn't built for comfort. He had only been able to sleep in one position, lying on his back. A knot in the vines that he had tied to keep the slats apart had dug into his back during the night. He carefully stretched – arms, legs, back, neck – to ease the cricks out of his body. He felt muscles expand and relax inside him with distinct clicks and twangs.

Ju-Long was still asleep. He retrieved his boots and shook them out, making absolutely sure nothing bitey or stingy had got in during the night. Then he pulled them on and closed his eyes blissfully at the feeling of his feet going into warm, dry leather.

The fire was almost out, just a pile of grey ashes and black fragments of wood. But part of it had been protected by the shelter and the ashes were fine and powdery, rather than just damp. He held his hand palm down over them, and felt a brush of warm air. Something in there was still putting out heat.

He knelt down with his face close to the pile and blew gently. A couple of the fragments glowed redly. He smiled and blew again. The red turned to orange. He rummaged quickly in the reserve pile of wood that Ju-Long had set aside, which had been kept dry by the shelter, and used a stick to push the embers together into a pile of their own. He blew on them again, and laid a couple of the smaller pieces over them.

"Shall I do that?" said a voice behind him. Ju-Long was sitting up, rubbing her eyes.

"Sure, thanks." He sat back and stood, still with a few residual twinges in his leg. His stomach had long forgotten the frogs and the bats, and he knew better than to try and cruise on empty. He would keep on burning those 1000 calories an hour until Mr Zhou was rescued, and his body wanted payment in advance. "I'll go and see if we've got anything to put on it."

Three of the five traps had been sprung during the night. The rocks or logs that he had carefully propped up and baited with bat guts had fallen down. And two of those had caught something. Each one had a jungle rat under it, killed instantly when the weights fell on top of them. He picked them up by their tails and carried them back to the camp. Before he went, he gave the last two traps a kick to set them off harmlessly. He and Ju-Long would be moving on, and there was no need to catch animals they weren't going to eat.

Ju-Long had stoked the fire up into a good blaze while he was gone. Now she stood a little away from it, feet slightly apart. She placed her hands together in front of her, then slowly moved them apart to hang by her side, again, casual but poised.

Slowly she brought her left leg up, bending it at the knee, then straightened it out and moved it forward so that she had taken one big step. With her hands held in front of her, palms facing out, she moved the weight of her body from one foot to the other.

Now, this Beck did know about. Tai chi. He had seen it done many times, though not often this close, and he had never tried it himself. He wondered if he should. He knew it had been developed as a martial art, but now it was used for exercise and for healing.

"I have done this every morning of my life," she said conversationally. She moved a hand slowly in front of her face, brought her body round and thrust the arm out. "It is the perfect way to bring balance back to your body, especially if you have spent a night in the jungle. Would you like to join me?"

Beck could easily have copied the movements, but somehow he knew he would just appear graceless and clumsy. Every movement she did seemed exactly right. She knew exactly where she was going to place her foot or her hand, and she did so.

"I won't, thanks. I'll get breakfast ready."

There was another reason. It was daylight again – time to be moving. Last night he could take time out for a lesson in *ki* because they had stopped for the day. Now, again, everything they did had to bring rescuing Mr Zhou a little bit closer.

He still kept one eye on her as he took his knife and a thin bamboo pole, and cut off two sharp bamboo skewers. With a rat in one hand and a skewer in the other, he pressed the skewer tip against the rat's fur and punctured the skin, then started to work it through the body, making sure he pushed it through the meat and carefully missing the guts.

Meanwhile her motions grew faster, more energetic, but still with that sense of total control. She jumped from one foot to the other, thrust her legs and arms out at imaginary attackers, and spun in circles on her feet. Then she slowed down again, her motions taking more and more time. Gradually she came to a complete stop, arms again at her sides, just as when she had started.

Beck wanted to applaud, but he wondered if it would be an insult. She had not been putting on a show. She had been doing something that was special and important to her, and his admiration wasn't what she had been after. But it had been a wonderful thing to watch – balanced and effortless.

She crouched down by the fire to warm her hands. He was holding the first rat over the flames on the end of the skewer, still complete with guts and fur."

"I'm afraid this is the best room service could come up with. On the plus side, we've got plenty of water to wash it down with."

As he had intended, their bottles were full to overflowing after the night's rain.

She looked puzzled.

"You are not going to skin and gut them first?"

He shook his head.

"Shouldn't need to. We'll let the fire do that."

He moved the rat closer and closer to the flames, until the fur started to singe. Not so close that it would catch fire. The smell of scorched rat fur was bitter and unpleasant, like burning hair, but after a while he could use another stick to scrape it away so that the rat's bare skin began to cook instead. He rotated the rat slowly so that all the fur got treated the same way and the rat was completely bald. Its skin slowly turned brown above the heat and its body slowly swelled, stretching the crisping skin tighter and tighter. The guts that Beck had left inside it were full of fluid which would be doing what any fluid does when heated – bubbling and steaming and expanding inside the rat.

"You see, you cook it in its skin, you keep all the nutrients in," he said. "Didn't do it with the bats because they were so small it makes no difference, but here, we're doing ourselves a favour."

"Until it goes pop."

"Yeah, well, we try to avoid that."

He took his knife and made a small prick in the rat's underside, just below its ribs, careful not to press too far. Then, still with just the tip of the knife, he sliced carefully down through the skin. The swelling guts spilled out of the cut, still intact. He could use his finger to scrape them out of the rat's body and drop them on the ground.

Beck held the rat over the fire again so that the heat could get into the body through the new hole and give the juices that were still leaking out a final sizzle. Then he passed it to Ju-Long.

"Rat on a stick!"

She nibbled it cautiously while he started to cook the second one.

"It tastes better than the bat," she said through a mouthful.

"Maybe it just had a more active and fulfilling life than hanging upside down all day in a dark, damp cave." He turned his rat slowly, to get an even singe on all the fur. "It's had regular exercise, roamed widely and eaten a well-balanced diet."

She looked thoughtfully at the body on its skewer. "Should I eat –"

"Just eat everything. Backbone, the lot. It'll crunch but it's the best way to get the nutrients out of the bones."

The best bit was the haunches, he found when his own turn came – the thick meat at the top of the rear legs. And between them were the kidneys, only the size of peas but full of iron and vitamins. He followed his own advice and crunched the backbone between his teeth. It tasted... not good, not bad, just like something that had never expected to be eaten. He pulled a face. He would not be ordering the rat backbone next time he was in a restaurant. But, out here in the jungle, the fact was that every bit of cooked rat inside him and Ju-Long would give them more energy to fulfil their mission for Mr Zhou.

On that basis... he looked at the two mostly eaten rat bodies. The heads were still intact because neither of them had fancied crushing the rat skulls with their molars. But, inside the skulls would be brains – more cooked meat.

He jammed his knife blade into the first skull and twisted it to crack the skull open. The brain inside it was black and knobbly, the size of a pea. He pried it out and popped it into his mouth. It tasted pungent and strong, but it was one more piece of cooked food that wouldn't go to waste.

He cut the other brain out for Ju-Long, and got up to stretch his legs. Cooked rat made him thirsty. He wanted to conserve the water they had collected in their bottles, so he went elsewhere.

He didn't even have to find a stream. There were plenty of natural bowls in the trees around them – places where the trunks and branches hadn't grown straight, and natural cavities had formed in the wood. They were all topped up with water from the night's rain.

If the water had been a day old, or more, Beck would have thought twice. Stuff would have started to grow in it that he didn't want in his stomach. Fresh water was different. He found the thinnest bamboo branch that he could and cut the ends off a section, so that he just had a hollow tube. Then he put the end into the nearest small pool and sucked. Fresh, clean water gushed into his mouth, slightly wood flavoured. After the rat, it was very refreshing.

Ju-Long washed her rat down the same way, and they were ready to move off: fed, watered and re-energised. They left the hammocks and shelters where they were. They weren't in any-one's way. But, there was one last duty to perform. After a good night's sleep and with a drink of water inside him, Beck felt he would be the best one to perform it.

"Um," he said. She looked at him expectantly, poised to start. "Yes?"

"I ... uh ... need ... The fire needs to be ..."

She looked at him, and at the fire. It had died down again to just a few glowing embers and a pile of ash. Suddenly her eyes went wide with understanding.

"Of course! Easier for a boy. I will wait for you ... over here."

She turned her back and pointedly walked away, leaving him to unzip and pee on the fire in his own good time.

"It only takes one small ember to start a fire," he said as he caught her up afterwards.

"Burning down the jungle we're walking through would be ... careless," she agreed.

They set off at a good place, following the river down the gorge. Beck remembered his thoughts of the night before: Mr Zhou, stuck on that ledge with the others, some of them injured. And he remembered the vow he had made.

We're coming, Mr Zhou. We're coming.

CHAPTER 26

It was hard to tell at first, with the jungle blocking their sight, but Beck soon became sure that the ground was sloping downwards again. The day before, they had climbed up a twenty metre cliff that blocked their way down the gorge. Ever since then they had been up above the river, able to head down the gorge but not to get close to the water.

But now it seemed to Beck that the noise of the river was growing louder and closer. They were on a very gentle slope. Out of curiosity he changed course to head for the sound of the river noise. A few minutes later, he stood at the edge of a very small cliff, no more than three or four metres high. He had been right. When he looked downstream, he could see that within another half mile they would be back at the same level as the river.

"It gets wider," Ju-Long said, looking in the same direction. Beck nodded. They couldn't see much more than that, because the river curved around a high headland. It was covered in jungle and outlined against thick clouds.

"And a wide river is a slow river," he said. "We might be able to put a raft together after all."

They soon came to the low piece of land. It was clear of trees. And ahead, the river sure enough curved around the headland. In front was a wide flat area of rocky pools and a beach of dark, gritty sand. The beach was covered with dead, discarded bits of wood, which was good news.

"The river has been much higher than it is now," Ju-Long pointed out. Beck nodded. That was how the wood had got onto the beach, stranded when the water went down again.

"So it's going down. And if it was this high recently then there might be fish trapped in the pools."

Ju-Long went to investigate while Beck stood at the edge of the river and looked across it.

The water was a rich, dark brown, coloured by sediment washed down from the hills. It no longer raged and foamed like it had upstream. The current wasn't forced between two narrow banks, so there was space for its energy to spread out a bit. It looked almost smooth.

Unfortunately it was still too fast. A floating branch moved past him at the speed of a steady jog. If he angled his head he could still see wide, flat ripples caused by hidden currents and obstacles beneath the surface.

He went back to Ju-Long, shaking his head.

"Still too risky for a raft, I reckon."

It would be great if they could move at the speed of the floating log. They would get downstream a lot more quickly, and it would be a smoother ride than before. Mr Zhou's rescue would suddenly be a lot closer. But, one good knock from a log or a rock could still tip them over. Then they would be in the water, out of their depth in a current that was too strong to swim against, and at the mercy of any other hidden danger. Beck had no intention of doing that again. No, they were going to stay on foot.

She was crouching by one of the pools.

"Well, if it's any help, I've found our next meal."

"Yeah?"

Beck crouched beside her and peered into the water. A freshwater crab was moving slowly sideways across an underwater rock, just below the surface. Its shell was spiky and pale grey against the darker stone. It was about the width of a pudding bowl, with four jointed legs sticking out on either side, and powerful claws held at the ready in front of it.

"Excellent! One of those each will do us nicely."

Crab meat was very rich and he guessed there would be enough on a couple like this one to keep him and Ju-Long going for a good while.

Ju-Long removed her coat, then rolled up her sleeves and lay on her front by the pool. She poised her hands over the water, then slowly reached into the pool, guiding her hand to the crab. It sensed the motion and spun around to face her, claws raised. She paused, and withdrew her hand.

She tried again, from another direction. Again, it sensed her coming. She took her hand and pursed her lips in frustration.

"I may just have to be pinched, but I would rather not be."

"Not if you can help it," Beck agreed. Like her he had taken off his coat. He lay next to her and reached down with his hand directly above the crab. No matter which way it now turned, it couldn't get its claws onto him. Then he pressed down quickly, pinning it against the rock. Now he could simply use his other hand to grab a back leg and lift it free of the water.

The crab twisted in its hand and waved its claws about vaguely, but it couldn't reach him with them to pinch.

"We need to keep them alive until we cook them," he said. "A dead crab goes poisonous almost immediately and no amount of cooking will fix it."

She nodded, and held the side pocket of his pack open for him. He dropped it in and zipped it up tight.

"How long can they survive out of water?" she asked.

"Long enough for us. As long as their gills are damp, they can get oxygen out of the water – but they don't have to be in water for that to happen. They can seal their gills off to stop them drying out, and they can store water in their own bodies. Clever little things. Okay, let's get another..."

He quickly caught a second one from another pool and dropped it into the other side pocket. The crabs had to be kept apart because he didn't know how well they would take to being forced into each other's company. Crabs could be aggressive towards each other, he knew, especially if they were both male.

So, the usual question where food was concerned: stop now and cook it, or cook it later when they stopped anyway? It was nine a.m. – not even mid-morning. The rats were probably still powering them.

He looked thoughtfully at the beach of the river, which stretched around the headland, and then at the headland itself.

"Let's set ourselves a target. I say we go up again, over that high ground. We'll rejoin the river on the other side. And we'll want a break at the top, so that's where we'll eat."

"That will save us a couple of miles," she agreed.

They drank, then refilled their bottles with fresh rain water from a small pool, and set off up the slope of the headland, leaving the river behind them. They were back in the jungle and now each step was noticeably higher than the one before it, so before long there was a good, steady throb in their legs. They saved their breath and didn't chat, just pausing now and again for a drink of water. The extra effort was making them sweat more than usual. It tried to evaporate off their bodies, but the humidity of the jungle kept it close to their skin. It was like being surrounded by their own personal steam baths.

But the air began to cool down again, and the first hints of a distinct, clean, resinous smell drifted down on the breeze. The trees were changing around them. Instead of the tightly packed vegetation further down the slope, they were sparser, and a lot of them were pines.

"Nearly there." Beck broke the no-talking rule to point it out. "Pines like to grow in thin, rocky soil – like you get at the top of steep slopes."

Another sign that the soil was thinning was more exposed rock. They passed between stony granite outcrops where the soil had weathered away, washed out by the rain, ultimately to join the river far below.

And then, without warning, they had left the trees behind them. They stood on the highest part of the headland with the river and jungle spread out before them.

CHAPTER 27

The first thing Beck noticed was the light. The clouds that had been so thick before were much thinner. He was high up enough to see right across the carpet of jungle, to the horizon, twenty or thirty miles away where beams of sunlight pierced the cloud and reached down to the ground. It would take a long time for the good weather to reach them, but it was the first sign that Typhoon Liliang might actually be blowing itself out.

He studied the view carefully, building a mind map of what lay ahead of them.

They were still in the gorge, just. If he looked behind him, he could see the walls towering up on either side. It was like standing between the pillars of a particularly tall gateway to a forbidding path.

But, ahead, downstream, the walls came down gradually to the ground. It was still hilly – the tree canopy went up and down in endless, rolling waves for as far as the eye could see. But they were no longer hemmed in by the gorge. The thickly wooded slopes were steep, but nowhere near vertical. The gorge had become a valley where the river did a series of long, slow S-bends over a stretch of many miles. The high ground inside each bend was a peninsula, almost like an island. Perhaps in another few thousand years they all really would be islands, as the river eroded the thin neck at their bases altogether. The headland where they stood was the highest of the series, letting Beck look down on the way ahead.

Directly in front of them, at the bottom of the slope, the river was wide and smooth. After the first bend he couldn't see the water any more, just the groove that the valley cut through the tree canopy. So, did it stay wide and smooth? He had no way of knowing. He had still gathered enough useful information to inform their journey for the rest of the day.

But there was one thing he couldn't see, and neither could Ju-Long.

"No settlements," she said, disappointment heavy in her voice. Mr Zhou had said there were settlements downstream. If there were, they must be in a dip because they couldn't see any sign of them from up here.

But that didn't mean they didn't exist.

"They don't have to be big," he pointed out. "All we need is a single, solitary phone, and I don't care if it's in huge great city or a fisherman's river shack by the river."

He checked his watch. It was now just past ten o'clock in the morning – the same time they had landed by helicopter the day before. What a twenty four hours. It was now four hours since they had woken up and breakfasted on cooked rat. "So, how about that crab for brunch?"

There was the perfect place for a camp nearby. A smooth, flat rock to build a fire on, surrounded by sun-warmed boulders to hold the breeze off. They worked together to gather up kindling and tinder and fuel. Ju-Long laid out a small circle of stones to hold the fire in and got it going with the fire steel, while Beck took the first crab out of its side pocket. It was still alive and well.

The only way to hold them without getting pinched was to dangle them by the back leg, but that way it was almost impossible to hold them steady to crack their shells. Instead Beck grabbed its claws, one in each hand so that it couldn't pinch him, and jammed them together. The pinchers fastened on each other, and Beck could hold it with one hand wrapped around both the interlocked claws at once. He swiftly cracked the shell open with the knife, held in his free hand, and levered the top off.

The crab's guts were a messy pile in the middle of its soft flesh, and he scooped them out. Around the edges of the shell were the gills, clammy little ridges like dead men's fingers. He got rid of them too. As well as being for breathing, the gills were the crab's filters – everything in the water around it went through them, and that included a lot of gunge. But what was left over – a shell full of white, tender flesh – that was just fine to eat.

Ju-Long picked up the second crab the same way as he had. She looked at it thoughtfully for a moment, considered, and then cracked its shell hard against a rock.

"*Hi!*"

The top came away as cleanly as if Beck had used his knife, and a lot more easily.

"Definitely learning to do that," he vowed.

They placed the shells over the fire to cook. The smell of rich, cooking food was delicious and made both their stomachs rumble. In a real emergency they could have eaten them raw but that was risky – any kind of shellfish could contain toxins that no one wanted inside them. Extreme vomiting was the nicest thing that could happen to you. Paralysis was a distinct possibility.

While Ju-Long cooked the crab, Beck wandered over to the nearest pine. He used his knife to cut away a patch of the tree's outer covering, which was sticky with resin, and exposed the moist, white inner bark.

"You could kill that tree," Ju-Long protested.

"Only if I take too much," She was right: trees need their bark just like humans need their skin – for protection, for waterproofing, for transporting gases and liquids. If he cut too much then it would be easy to inflict irreparable harm. But trees are also resilient and he could take a little.

"Most bits of a pine are edible," he said conversationally as he tucked chunks of the white bark away in his pack for later. "You can eat the nuts, though you have to get them out of their cones first. You can boil the needles up to make a good tea. And the bark is full of vitamin C and A. So we'll keep this for later."

They sat down on rocks on either side of the fire and tucked in with enjoyment, using their fingers to scoop the cooked flesh out of the shell and feeling its richness go into their stomachs. Beck pulled the claws off his crab and used a rock to crack them open. Some of a crab's best meat was in the claws and he wasn't going to let it go to waste.

Ju-Long went suddenly still.

"Beck. Do not move."

He froze, one hand with a claw in it half way to his mouth. Her tone was not one to argue with, and Beck trusted her judgement.

"What's the –" he began, and then his question was answered. An angry, high pitched *hiss* behind him that could only come from one kind of creature.

"What type?" he asked quietly, still not moving his head. She peered past him.

"I think, a cobra. Very deadly. About one metre behind you."

CHAPTER 28

Hiss-s-s...

Beck felt the noise rather than heard it. Outwardly he didn't move a muscle; inwardly his heart pounded. *Go on, snakey, we all know you hate vibrations and I must be vibrating this hill down...*

Hiss-s-s...

It had to be very close behind him. It must have been sheltering in a crack in the rocks, until the two humans came along and disturbed it. He and Ju-Long weren't the only living things to have found the rocks a pleasantly warm and dry place to rest.

"How long is it?" he asked, still keeping his voice quiet.

"About a metre."

So, it was an adult, in full possession of all its abilities, more aggressive than a youngster. And while most snakes would happily avoid humans if they heard you coming, the cobra was one of the exceptions. Cobras could attack.

"Is the hood up?"

"Yes. And the front of its body."

Beck closed his eyes. *Oh, great.*

When a cobra lifted its forebody off the ground, and spread its hood out on either side of its head, it meant one thing. *Back off! I have poisonous fangs, I know how to use them, and I don't like you.*

He quickly ran through what he knew about cobra venom in his head. Haemotoxins and neurotoxins combined – meaning, it clotted your blood into black pudding *and* it attacked your nervous system, so even if the blood could be fixed, the rest of your body shut down anyway. Most snakes just settled for one or the other, but not the cobra, no. Two ways to kill you – twice as hard to survive in the middle of the jungle.

But he also knew that even a cobra would only attack if it felt it had a point to make. Like, if they were desperate or felt trapped, or just wanted you off their territory. By camping down here, he and Ju-Long had probably managed to tick both boxes – it regarded this little patch of rocks as its territory, and it felt trapped by them, with rocks behind it and humans in front.

"Okay. Step back," he said calmly. He still hadn't turned his head to look at the snake. It was only in his imagination that the cobra was growing larger and larger, poised to plunge its fangs into his back.

Ju-Long stepped away by a couple of paces.

"Further. I want a clear run."

Ju-Long moved herself a few metres away. Slowly, casually, with no sudden movements, Beck drew his legs beneath him and tensed.

"Okay, snakey," he said. "Shame you can't understand a word I'm saying, because I'm going to move away in three ... two ... one ..."

All his energy pushed into a single thrust of his legs, leaping away from his seat and over the fire. He told himself that the feeling of fangs snapping closed behind him was only his imagination.

He stopped by Ju-Long and drew several long, slow breaths to calm himself and let his pounding heart slow down. Then he turned around.

The cobra still had its hood up, but it was lowering its head and starting to look away. All it had wanted was for him to push off. It must have only been a few centimetres behind him when he jumped. Its body was coiled, filling up the gap between the rock where he had been sitting and the larger boulder behind it.

Now, from a safe distance, he could admire it for the wonderful creature it was. Its body was a dark metallic grey, lined with interlocking scales that moved together like a smooth, mechanical mesh. Its underside was a continuous, rippling row of single scales that stretched like bands across its body. Its throat was creamy white and there were touches of red in the scales of its hood – like it thought the extra warning was actually needed when the hood went up. If the snake did bite anyone, no one could say they hadn't been told.

Beck had killed snakes before. Many. Such as a Bushmaster, that time in Colombia when he had been chasing drug traffickers in the jungles of Colombia. It had been a threat to him and his friends, and he had enjoyed eating it afterwards. Snakes were good eating – pure protein, if the opportunity presented itself.

But this wasn't a threat any more, and as long as it would let them retrieve their crabs then they didn't need to eat anything else. And the Bushmaster, he had killed with a single blow of a heavy machete that could just lop through its muscular body. His present knife was too small for that job, and the snake probably wouldn't want to stand still for him while he did it.

In short, this snake was getting away, and Beck was quite glad of it. But he and the snake still had unfinished business. There were two discarded crab shells, still with meat in them. As far as Beck was concerned, the snake could go hunt its own.

He sidled closer again, ignoring Ju-Long's stifled gasp of warning. The snake half lifted its head, but the shells were only a quick grabbing distance away. Beck snatched them up and quickly retreated.

They finished off quickly and wiped sticky, food stained hands on the wet ground. Beck looked thoughtfully at the fire.

The snake was still curled up next to it and there was no way he was peeing on those embers, even if the encounter with the snake had made him want to do exactly that. But they had built it on rock so there was nothing else to burn, and the circle of stones that surrounded it would prevent the embers from drifting. It should be safe to leave it. They would leave its warmth to the cobra as a gift.

They were at the top of the headland and the stupendous view was still in front of them. More sun was coming out, spreading out across the carpet of rolling hills. Gentle tendrils of mist were rising up off the tree canopy and tumbling down into the valleys. A mile in front of them, and a hundred metres below, the river cut across their course. It looked so brown and dark up close, but from up here it was a silver band that wound its way into the trees to disappear.

But when Beck looked back the way they had come, the sky was still dark with dense cloud. The typhoon had not yet passed for Mr Zhou and the others. For all he knew, the remains of that ledge could be crumbling away even as they sat and ate their cooked crab.

"Time to go," he said. They started down the slope, back towards the river. Back towards salvation.

CHAPTER 29

It took most of an hour to get back down to the river on the far side of the headland. The rocky high ground where they had stopped had been almost bare of trees and foliage, apart from a few pines. Before long, though, they were back in the jungle again, moving more slowly. Even so, Beck estimated that when they reached the river, even though they had paused for a meal and encountered the snake, they would have saved a couple of hours. It would have taken much longer to follow the river around the curve.

Shortly before they reached the river, a fallen tree blocked their way. For once, Beck didn't change course to go around it. It was only noon – there was a lot of day left and he didn't know when their next meal would be.

He felt for his knife and pulled the blade out.

"Let's take five," he said. Ju-Long looked puzzled.

"Five what?"

"It's an expression." He stopped at the tree and studied it. Lying down, it was half as high as he was. The bark was covered with clumps of moss and clung loosely to the trunk like the large scales of some giant lizard. He pried with the knife blade into one of the cracks and lifted the bark away.

Bingo! A couple of fat, wriggly grubs tried desperately to crawl for shelter. The biggest was almost the size of his thumb.

They were pale white with bodies made of circular segments. Just what he needed.

He picked one up and showed it to Ju-Long. She looked at it in bafflement.

"What about it?"

"Part of our thousand calories an hour. Grazing as you go along is just as important as eating a meal at regular intervals. Now, if this one had black spots below the skin, or any kind of colour, or hairy bits, that would be bad. But as it is..."

He tilted his head back and dropped it into his mouth. One crunch, and then he swallowed it whole. Unless he knew exactly what he was dealing with – like, say, an Australian witchetty grub, which tasted of eggs and nuts – that was the best way to avoid the foul taste. Just get it into his stomach, as quickly as possible.

"Want one?" he offered. He held the other one out.

Her bafflement had changed to horror. Now it was slowly being replaced with a look of reluctant interest.

"Not... especially." But she picked it up, held it thoughtfully, then crunched and swallowed. "I presume that did me good."

"Oh, all kinds." He looked down and pulled back some more bark, and soon found even more of the little wrigglers. Some of them were heading for shelter under other pieces of bark. "We shouldn't let them go to waste..."

Soon after, with slightly fuller stomachs, they passed through a grove of thick bamboo and came out onto the river bank again. There was a small strip of shoreline between the trees and the water.

Here, the river ran smooth and even. Somewhere in the bend that they had bypassed, it had hit something which had taken all the force and anger out of it. The raging torrent upstream was a distant memory.

Beck still had the view from the high ground fresh in his mind. They were on the outside edge of the first in a couple of giant S-bends that curved majestically out of sight downstream. So, the ground he was looking at dead ahead was another headland like the one they had climbed, though the trees seemed much thicker on it, all the way to the top. It would be dense jungle. And whether they went around it or over it, there would be another one like it after.

Beck pursed his lips thoughtfully as he looked down at the water, with a lump of wood in his hand. Then he drew his arm back and threw it out into the channel as far as it would go. It hit the water with a splash and bobbed to the surface. It spun slowly as it went, but it wasn't rushing and it wasn't being buffeted by hidden rocks and currents. The water was safer to get into. He guessed it was doing somewhere between four and five miles per hour – faster than on foot.

There was one more thing to check before he made his mind up.

"Are there alligators in this river?"

"Mr Zhou says that Chinese alligators are only found in the Yangtze River. That is further north and east – so, no, they will not be here."

He turned his head and gazed back at the bamboo grove they had just come through. He allowed himself a smile of anticipation as he did the calculations in his head.

"Okay," he said after a moment. "Let's do it."

"Do what?"

"Build a raft!"

CHAPTER 30

"**A**re you sure?" Ju-Long asked. "Do we have the time?"

"Well, that's the consideration, isn't it?" He put his hands on his hips and looked ahead. "It will take, maybe three hours to put the raft together. So the question is, how far would we get in two or three hours on foot?" He looked at his watch: a little after one p.m. it would be four by the time they finished building, with three more hours of daylight after that. Where would they be by sunset if they just kept walking now? Would the raft get them further in the same time?

She looked ahead and estimated.

"If we walk around this curve, and then climb the next headland – that could certainly be two or three hours of effort."

He nodded.

"And then we would have to get down the other side of the headland – and we don't know what that's like. Even if it's a nice, smooth, gentle slope, it could take another hour to join the river again. And if it's a sheer cliff, it will take longer. And who knew what lies after that?"

"Whereas, the time it takes to build a raft now will be paid back by an efficient, smooth ride all the way down the river," she said with a big smile. She had caught up with his reasoning.

"With minimum energy expended as the river does all the work," Beck added. Well, until the next obstacle."

"And how do we..." Ju-Long began. Then: "Let me guess. Bamboo?"

"We're in China – what else?" Beck said with a grin. He headed back to the grove at a fast pace. "It's the best thing for making rafts. The stalks are divided into waterproof compartments. It will float whatever happens."

The bamboo stalks in the nearest cluster were too thin for what he had in mind. He could close either of his hands around them. He wanted the thickest poles they could get.

He found the right ones growing a short distance away. He guessed the largest ones were maybe fifteen centimetres across, and they went up to four metres or more in length. Try as he might, he couldn't get his fingers round them even with both hands. Perfect.

"I guess even you would struggle with your hand chop thing?" he said regretfully. She looked at the pole and nodded in agreement.

"Too thick. But you will need vine?"

"A lot," he confirmed. "The thin, twisty type, to use for rope. Can you –"

"As much as we need!" she said with a smile.

She set off into the trees to begin her task. Beck stepped back and surveyed the grove, doing the calculations in his head. How many poles did he need?

Ten would be a good, round number. Ten fifteen-centimetre poles tied together would make a raft a metre and a half wide – that should be room for him and Ju-Long. It wouldn't be comfortable, but this wasn't being built for comfort, just speed.

But then, he would need more poles, because a single layer would be too flexible. The poles would be tied together so they wouldn't move apart, but there would be nothing to stop them rubbing up and down. If the layer was A-deck then he needed B-deck above it, so that he could tie the two together and they would reinforce each other. They would make a sturdy platform. So, say, eight more poles, tied together so that the poles of B-deck lay in the gaps between the poles of A-deck. Eighteen in total. He crouched down and started to saw away at the base of the first pole.

As he cut each one, he dragged it a short distance away to the river's edge so that he could lay them down, side by side. The poles weren't perfect cylinders – the bamboo stalks were knobbly with a small ridge at the start of each section – but they went together well enough. A-deck would be somewhere between one and a half metres to two metres wide. That would do for width.

But it was way too long. Most of the poles were at least four metres. All of them tapered off towards the top, sprouting into shoots and leaves. He wanted them to be more or less the same width all the way, and he certainly didn't need the leaves at the end. He set out chopping them all off at the three metre mark. This served a double purpose, because in a few cases he could use the chopped off section as part of B-deck.

All the cutting of wood reminded him of the pine bark in his bag. He laid the fragments out on a rock so that they could each nibble at them as they worked.

He assembled the two decks side by side on the edge of the river until he had enough for what he needed. Two decks, which would be about three metres long and two wide. But to make them secure, the poles would need to be tied together. There were a couple of ways he could do that. He could loop vine around each one in turn – or, even better, he could thread the vine through holes he had drilled through each pole. Say, one at each end, and one in the middle for stability. That meant the bamboo section in the middle of each pole would no longer be watertight, but the buoyancy of the rest of the pole would still hold it up.

Beck plunged the tip of his knife into the first pole and worked the blade back and forth, twisting it round to cut a circular hole.

He only had to cut through a centimetre of wood before he was through to the hollow interior, but he had to do this six times for each pole, once on either side at the bottom, middle and top. He began to suspect it might take as long as cutting the poles down in the first place.

"I think I have all the vine," Ju-Long said. She came up to him, peeking around the sides of a massive vine bundle. "Most of the vine in the jungle. What else can I do?"

"You can take the ones I've done and start to tie them together. Thanks." She nodded and knelt down by the first poles of A-deck.

"It's actually fun to try and make a raft," she commented as she pulled a length of vine free.

"Of course. It makes you feel alive," Beck replied.

"Feel alive, stay alive!" she said, quick as a flash. Beck laughed.

Ju-Long selected the thickest vines to push through each hole, threading the poles together like beads on an abacus. To stop them sliding back and forth, she looped each vine around the pole once before pushing it through the holes in the next one.

Pole by pole, the two decks came together. By the time Beck was done, A-deck was complete and B-deck just needed the last couple of pieces. When both were done, they lifted B-deck on top of A-deck and pulled vine up through the gaps between poles, tying the ends and binding the two decks together.

At last the two of them could stand back and admire their handiwork. Beck hadn't been far off on his time estimate. A shade under three hours.

"China has a space station," Ju-Long said unexpectedly. Beck looked at her questioningly. "There are Chinese astronauts living in space right now. It is an amazing technological challenge and my country has overcome it. So, why do I feel so pleased that we have built a simple raft?"

Beck laughed again. "Because it's all relative, and doing something with your own hands always feels better. It's how we're made – part of where we come from. All of us are survivors, really. Come on, let's test it out."

They lifted it easily and slid it into the shallows of the river. Beck had tied one end of a vine onto one of the poles and he kept the other in his hand, so the current wouldn't carry it off. It bobbed nicely, riding almost completely above the water.

Beck turned the long end of the raft towards himself, and handed the end of the safety line to Ju-Long. Then he stepped cautiously out into the water and climbed on board. The vines and the poles creaked as they stretched and rubbed together, adjusting to the new weight they had to carry, but they held. His weight pushed A-deck further down into the water but the bamboo was amazingly buoyant. B-Deck didn't get wet at all.

He crawled as far forward as he could, muscles tensing for balance, before he sensed that if he went any further then the raft might flip over and pitch him into the shallows. He pulled back and stayed on his knees in the middle. The raft rocked and bucked beneath him, but now he didn't feel in any danger of it tipping over. As long as he and Ju-Long stayed near the centre line, it should be safe.

He lowered himself back off the raft and waded to the bank.

"Just a couple more things and we can go."

The couple more things were a pair of long, straight bamboo poles, one for each of them.

"It's the only way we'll be able to steer," he said. "There's no point in a rudder because we'll basically be moving at the same speed as the water and a rudder wouldn't work. If we try to paddle too much we might tip it over. So we stick as close as we can to the bank and we use these to push ourselves along."

"Sounds like a plan," Ju-Long agreed.

She crawled onto the raft first, going down to the forward end. Beck passed her the poles, and then in one move he climbed on board and kicked away from the bank.

The raft rocked as he took his place and the vines creaked some more. The combined weight of two human bodies drove it further into the water and little waves splashed up through the gaps in the decks, but Beck had expected that. The important thing was, they were afloat and moving.

Straight into a patch of water moving at a higher speed than the water nearer the bank. The front of the raft hit it and they began to spin.

CHAPTER 31

"**O**kay, let's hold it steady..."

They pushed their poles down to stop the raft's rotation. They were already moving at the speed of a fast walker on the bank and the touch of the pole against the river bed almost knocked it out of Ju-Long's hand. It took a little time and practice to coordinate their pole work but before long they had the hang of it. The raft needed constant nudges to keep it away from the bank.

"We need to stick close to the bank," Beck called. "The current will try to throw us out into the middle of the river, where it'll be too deep to paddle."

The beach where they had built the raft was on the outside edge of the river's curve, where the water flowed fastest. The outside curve of this bend became the inside curve of the next one as the S-bend continued. The inside curve was where the water ran the slowest and most smoothly. If they could get there and not be thrown out into deeper water, they would be able to pole themselves along gently.

More water slapped up through B-deck, and the raft bucked beneath them. They were at the place where the current around the outside curve was strongest and roughest. It was hitting the shore and bouncing back in waves. The raft was resisting their guidance. The river was bigger and stronger than they were, and it wanted to do what the river dictated.

And, as Beck had foreseen, the river wanted to take them over to the other side. The raft span around again so that it was travelling sideways, and it began to follow the current away from the bank.

Beck quickly moved his pole over to the raft's left hand side and dug it into the river bed.

"You keep pushing on the right," he said. Together, pushing either end of the raft in different directions, they made it turn round again so that it was travelling forwards.

"Now switch over to the left, like me."

Ju-Long brought her pole over and they both pushed in. A small wave smacked over the front of the raft and soaked their knees, but it quickly drained away through the gaps in the deck. Another advantage of the raft, Beck thought, was that it couldn't fill up with water and sink.

And then they were safely into the current around the inside curve. The raft travelled at a smooth and sedate pace, though it was impossible just to sit back and enjoy the cruise, always having to be poised for the next correction. The forested slopes of the next headland moved past them faster than they could have marched. Yes, Beck thought, the raft had been the right choice to make. It more than justified the time spent constructing the thing.

The biggest problem of being pretty well at the same level as the surface of the water was that you couldn't see what lay ahead. Anything like a rock sticking up – that would be visible. But if the river went *down*, that was another matter. Beck had been white water rafting and he knew how sometimes the water can just fall away in front of you. In the right conditions, or rather the wrong conditions, it could be invisible to someone low down. It would be quite easy for the river to drop down into rapids and for them not to see it coming.

Of course, deliberately going down the rapids was the whole point of white water rafting. But their bamboo raft was built for survival, not for fun, and it wouldn't cope if they hit rapids. Beck had had one taste of that on this journey and that was quite enough for him.

"We need to keep listening," he told Ju-Long. He didn't take his eyes off the river. "Anything that sounds like rapids, water-falls, water hitting something…"

"I understand," she said, without turning round. "Four ears are better than two."

Water loves to make a noise. White water might be hard to see from this level, but it would be very easy to hear.

They were coming around the first bend. A new stretch of river was opening up and they were seeing it for the first time. From up on the headland, Beck had been able to see the river channel but not the details. He redoubled his survey of what lay ahead.

The river was still wide and smooth, a brown, glistening plain between two slopes of thick jungle. But now they were coming out of the inside curve of the first bend, the river wanted to throw them out into the middle of the channel.

"Okay," he said, "we need a nudge on the left to keep us near the bank…"

Then Beck's eyes caught something up ahead. He narrowed them and craned his neck, leaning up as far as he safely could without unbalancing the raft.

Up ahead, for the second half of the S-bend, the inside curve again became the outside curve. And this one had rocks. White water splashed hard against a shoreline of boulders. If they stayed in this current, the raft would be dashed to bits.

"Right." His eyes darted back and forth across the channel. "We need to cross over to the other side to be on the inside of the next bend and away from those rocks. And we need to do it quickly." If they went much further, the raft would be too close to the rocks to make any difference when they crossed over. They would miss the opposite bank. "One, two, three, *push!*"

They jammed their poles in on the right hand side of the bank, and kept pushing. The raft needed no convincing – it was happy to spin out into the deeper water of the middle channel. In just a few moments they were out of the poles' depth and no longer had any means to control their direction. They could only go where the river took them.

The water grew rougher, and more of it splashed under and over them. The raft began to spin more quickly and they had no way of stopping it. They hunkered low to keep their balance as it turned sideways on and drifted downstream. Beck watched the opposite bank pass by with bated breath. Was it getting closer? The idea of pushing off so hard had been to give them momentum that would carry them over. But the river might have had other ideas – it could just be taking them downstream, slap bang into those rocks he had wanted to avoid...

The raft spun abruptly round so that now it was travelling backwards.

"Okay!" Beck said quickly. "See if we're in depth!"

They hadn't hit anything but that sudden change of direction meant something had happened. The front end had moved into slower moving water while the back end kept going quickly. So, it had flipped around. And that slower water might mean it was shallower here.

The water tugged at the pole in Beck's hands as he thrust it down, probing for the river bed. And there it was – with his arms outstretched and his hands as close to the water as they could get, he felt the pole tap against something.

"Got it! Push!"

The tips of the poles bit in, more and more as the water grew shallower. They pushed the raft around again to bring Ju-Long back to the front. Beck breathed a sigh of relief. The water was kinder and gentler here, and more importantly, there were no rocks. He glanced across the river. Now he could hear the water dashing against the rocks across the width of the river. It was a pleasant, peaceful sound, but one he was very happy to be hearing at a distance.

They poled gently along the river's left bank. Here the jungle's foliage came right down to the water and many trees overhung it, with vines and branches dropping down almost to the surface. Although Beck was reluctant to move away from the bank, they had to head out into the channel slightly to avoid the overhanging branches. The river grew deeper quite quickly and suddenly his pole barely scraped the bottom.

They came around the next bend and once again a new vista of river opened up – smooth and unbroken.

Beck narrowed his eyes again. Smooth – in fact too smooth. There was a dead straight line in the water about a hundred metres ahead, like someone had sliced through the river with a fine knife from left to right. He knew exactly what that meant, and his ears confirmed it, filling with the noise of foaming water dashing against solid stone. Rapids, dead ahead, which would smash the raft and them to pieces.

CHAPTER 32

"**Q**uick! Get us to the bank!"

It was easier said than done. The overhanging foliage blocked their way back to the bank. They dug their poles in and pushed. The front of the raft nudged into a branch that hung into the water. The branch bent, and then pushed them back. By the time they got control again, they were several metres nearer the rapids.

Eventually Beck had to put his pole down, and bend double, and grab a branch to pull them in. Leaves and twigs scraped against his head and back.

But suddenly there was a clear spot, between the bank and the overhang. Ju-Long gave a last thrust with her pole and they touched the ground. Beck quickly jumped up with the safety line in his hand. He tied it to a tree and gave Ju-Long a hand as she clambered to the shore.

Five minutes later they stood on the bank downstream, at the edge of the rapids. White water foamed and fell for fifty metres or more, down a shallow slope studded with boulders and rocks. If it had been on dry land then the slope would have been quite gentle, something they barely noticed. But the rushing water made it lethal. They would not have stood a chance if they went over it.

"Okay," he said sadly. "I'd say we did about four hours foot journey in half an hour, so that's still pretty darn good."

"Could we carry the raft past the rapids?"

"Hmm." Beck turned to look along the bank in either direction. The jungle was just as thick as before. And, though the river dropped down through the rapids, the bank stayed at the same level, which meant that beyond the rapids it was about five metres higher than the water. The river curved again, so he couldn't see more than a hundred metres or so past the rapids. They might have to carry the raft quite some distance to get it back into the river, through dense undergrowth that would constantly be getting in their way. And while bamboo might be a light wood, and they could just about pick the raft up between them, it wasn't light enough to carry for great distances. They would wear themselves out for sure.

"No," he decided reluctantly. "It's done its job. We're back on foot for now."

He squinted along the river. The jungle ran along it for as far as he could see. As did the cliff.

And suddenly, out of nowhere, came a thought like a blow to the head. *We're not going to make it.* The river just went on and on. There was no sign of civilisation ...

No! Beck told himself. *Never lose hope, and just kick negative thoughts away.*

They were like junk food to the survivor – tempting, but damaging. A survivor had to maintain focus and hope, and never, ever give up.

He knew they could do this. He had adventures behind him that proved it, in jungles and deserts and mountains and frozen wastes around the world. They had got this far. They had spent a night in the jungle. They had found food. They had just used human ingenuity to take a four hour chunk out of their journey.

But knowledge always comes second to spirit. However much knowledge you have, it is no good if you don't have the determination to use it.

So, he determined that they were going to get through this. If they stayed alive and healthy then they would reach help. It was inevitable.

Eventually.

"We can spend a second night in the jungle," said Ju-Long as though she were reading his thoughts.

"We can," he said grimly. "Can Mr Zhou?" He shook his head with worry.

She put her hand on his to stop him. Her head was cocked and she gazed blankly into the distance.

"Listen."

He froze, straining his ears. There was the usual rustle of leaves in the wind, the distant sound of the rapids...

...and a very faint pulsing sound, a regular noise that could not be natural. It could only be a machine.

"I think it's a boat!"

As one, they ran towards the bend in the river, downstream from the rapids.

Hurrying through the jungle broke all Beck's rules and the jungle was quick to remind him why. Branches hit against his face and vines twined around his feet. He risked breaking something until he forced himself to slow down. Take it easy, slow but sure, even though every cell in his body wanted to hurry and catch that boat before it went away again. Sometimes the press of vegetation meant he had to move away from the cliff edge. He couldn't see the boat – had no idea where it was. It could have already turned around...

They came out of the trees at the top of the cliff on the bend, and stared up and down the river. And there it was, in the middle of the channel, chugging its way upstream towards the rapids. They had run past it in the jungle – it was further upstream than they were now. It was narrow and pointed, four or five metres long. He couldn't tell how many people might be in it.

"Hey!" he shouted. He waved his hands above his head. "Hello!"

Beside him, Ju-Long began to shout in Chinese.

Beck realised the noise of the rapids was drowning out their voices. They hurried along the bank, as close as they could get to the edge, shouting and waving.

Now Beck could see there were at least two people on board. One was at the stern, holding onto the tiller to steer. The other stood in the front, hauling in a net. The engine was in a box in the middle of the boat, chugging loudly enough that neither man could hear them.

"Over here!" Beck shouted. "We need help!"

Ju-Long continued to shout in her own language, waving her arms frantically.

The man had pulled the net in, and Beck felt relief gush inside him as the boat began to turn towards them.

It kept turning. The boat wasn't coming to them – it was turning around to head back downstream. The rapids were as far as it could go. The engine surged a little, the chugs coming more frequently as the steersman throttled up.

"*No!*" he yelled. "Don't go! We need your help..."

Ju-Long shouted even more loudly, then went quiet.

"They can't hear us properly. They're too far away." She turned away. "We will have to follow them."

"Maybe..."

Beck shot a last look at the boat. If it was too far away now for them to be heard clearly, that wasn't going to change. It was going downstream and it had sped up. Perhaps the crew wanted to be home for tea.

They couldn't race it through the jungle. It would move faster and only get further away. They would never get nearer than they were now.

"Right," he said. He peered down at the water. There were rocks at the base of the cliff, and if he jumped from here then he probably wouldn't clear them. He would miss them if he took a running jump, and hit the water instead, but there wasn't space for that.

He looked around for what he wanted – a tree whose trunk was covered in vines, all climbing up to borrow its height and reach the sun. Some were tangled in the branches above, some dangled back down again, almost to the ground. And the branches overhung the river. He took hold of a vine and yanked. It held.

"Okay. Here goes."

She gasped.

"No! Beck, wait..."

He wasn't going to wait. There wasn't any choice. He gripped the vine, paced back as far as the trees would allow, then ran forward and flung himself into the air.

With hands and legs firmly clamped onto the vine, he swung out as far as it would go. He risked a look down and saw that he had passed over the rocks, for a split second. There was only water below him now, until he swung back again. And so, in that split second, he let go.

It was do or die.

CHAPTER 33

The river blurred beneath the helicopter's blades. Beck and Ju-Long stood behind the pilot with headphones clamped over their ears, plugging them into the comms system so they could be heard over the engine noise. Beck strained his eyes ahead through the windshield. They had been told to come up to the front to help navigate. On the thickly tree covered slopes of the gorge, it would be easy for the pilots to miss the ledge and its stranded party unless they knew where they were going.

It had been the motion that had caught the fishermen's eye – the sight of two young people jumping off a cliff. Ju-Long had followed immediately after Beck, swinging out on the same vine to clear the base of the cliff and drop into the water.

The fishermen had hauled them on board and Ju-Long had told their story – the men spoke no English. Straightaway they had throttled up to max and headed downstream for their village. More importantly, one of them had a phone. He had got in touch with the authorities the moment they were within signal range while their new passengers wrapped up in borrowed blankets and spread their clothes on deck to dry out. The men had given them a hot meal of noodles in sauce which they had both wolfed down.

So, by the time they got to the village, the helicopter was there waiting for them on the ground, with its engines running and a rescue crew in the cabin – a team of Chinese men who looked very professional and capable in proper climbing kit. It took off the moment they were on board, heading back to the gorge.

The headland where they had met the cobra loomed ahead, and within minutes it had passed beneath them. Beyond it Beck could see the shore where they had caught the crabs. After that, the trees were too thick to recognise landmarks, but he could see how the gorge ahead got higher and narrower. He could take in the whole scope of their journey just by moving his eyes.

The pilot pulled up slightly as they passed into the gorge itself. Beck remembered how he had looked back into it from the ground, and had thought that it looked like the gateway to somewhere. It still felt a bit like that now. It was close to six o'clock and sunset wasn't far away. The gorge was already dim. But he was keeping his vow. He hadn't had to spend another night in the jungle, and it looked like neither would Mr Zhou.

"There –"

"Look –"

Beck and Ju-Long spoke simultaneously. She had seen the pile of fresh rocks at the base of the gorge – the landslide that had killed Mr Muller and stranded the rest of them. He had seen a flash of bright colour near the top of the gorge. And now he looked closer he could see human figures up there, waving.

The helicopter slowed, and stopped, and hovered in mid-air. Then it started to rise vertically until it was level with the ledge, about ten metres from the top of the cliff.

And there were the trekkers, Mr Zhou and the rest, waving and shouting with joy. They must have raided everyone's backpacks for the brightest clothes they could find, and strung them out in a line as a banner that couldn't be missed.

But Beck noticed the fresh earth at the front of the ledge. He was sure it was more eroded than the last time he had seen them. Everyone was hanging back at the rear of the ledge, next to the cliff, away from the drop. And even as he looked, a piece the size of a washing machine broke away and tumbled down.

There was a fierce chatter of Chinese in his earphones, and immediately the helicopter dipped its nose and surged ahead, away from the ledge. Beck clutched the back of the pilot's seat for balance. The conversation continued – the pilots in the front and the rescuers in the back, talking loud and fast.

Ju-Long lifted one of Beck's earphones up so she could shout into his ear.

"They are afraid the vibration from the helicopter will cause even more damage. They can't hover and pick people up. They will have to find somewhere to land."

Beck nodded his understanding.

But, finding somewhere to land was easier said than done. The helicopter pulled up over the jungle above and flew slowly, all eyes peeled for a break in the tree canopy. Beck hoped they wouldn't have to go back to the clearing where the trekking party had been set down before this all began. That had been the better part of an hour's trek from the ledge. If they landed there and headed through the jungle, it could be after dark before they arrived.

Then the helicopter tilted as the pilot saw a spot and headed for it. It was a little bit of high ground, rocky like the place they had stopped for their meal, and the trees were thin. It was still too rough to touch down, but the pilot was able to hover a metre above the ground. The rescue crew leapt out, bodies bent over beneath the downwash from the blades, and started to unload their equipment.

Beck and Ju-Long went back into the cabin and helped pass things down. But when they tried to jump down to the ground themselves, one of the rescue team held his hand in Beck's face and gave him a volley of Chinese orders. Beck didn't need a translation – it was essentially, *stay here, kid, and let the grown-ups handle it.*

But, after everything they had been through to get help, he didn't want to let it rest there.

"Tell him we can help carry equipment!" he called to Ju-Long over the noise of the engines. "And time is of the essence if we're going to do this before dark!"

She passed the message on and he considered it for a second, before nodding abruptly. Beck quickly leapt out and shouldered a pack before anyone could change their mind. Ju-Long was close behind.

They stayed bent double as they hurried away from the artificial gale of the helicopter, then straightened up as it rose into the air again. Without a word, the small party quickly set off into the jungle, guided by the leader's compass bearing.

It took twenty minutes to emerge at the top of the gorge, above the ledge. The leader made the others stand back while he leaned over and had a shouted conversation with Mr Zhou below. Then he barked some orders at his men and they busily began to erect a pair of tripods, snapping metal poles together and digging them in at the top of the cliff. Another man slung a couple of rope loops around a pair of trees behind the tripods. Each loop had a pulley attached to it. They threaded climbing ropes through the pulleys, and over the top of the tripods, and attached stretchers to the other ends. Then the stretchers were lowered over the cliff, down to the trekkers. A couple of the rescue team also abseiled down the ropes to help at the other end.

Beck bit his lip in frustration. He wasn't a professional or a member of the team. The rescuers weren't going to let him near the equipment. After a day and a half of non-stop activity, always driving himself on to help Mr Zhou, here he was, stuck and not able to do anything.

The men started to haul on the ropes of both tripods. After a few minutes a pair of stretchers were pulled into view, one with a boy on, one with a girl. They were laid on the ground while the rescue crew's medic looked them over. The boy's head was bandaged and he checked that quickly. The girl was clutching her arm and her face was white. They exchanged a few words, and then he began to splint it. Meanwhile the stretchers were lowered back down.

Everything was very smooth and efficient, and Beck had no cause to complain. Except that...

Say it took five minutes to bring each trekker up, then lower the stretcher back down again. He did a quick count in his head. There were nineteen people down there – eighteen teenagers and Mr Zhou. Five minutes each for nineteen people was ninety five minutes. Over an hour and a half.

But there were two stretchers, so halve that. Still nearly fifty minutes – almost an hour. He gave the sky a quick check, and looked at his watch to confirm it. They really did not have an hour of daylight left.

The rescue leader had eyes too, of course. He spoke into the radio, and a moment later they heard the sound of the helicopter returning. It hovered above, not close enough to set off any more falls, and suddenly the scene was lit bright as day by its searchlight.

Shouts of alarm made Beck and Ju-Long look round. Ju-Long translated.

"The ledge! It is collapsing!"

CHAPTER 34

They hurried over to the cliff edge until suddenly their way was blocked by one of the rescuers. He held up a hand and barked stern orders in Chinese. Beck could understand without being told and he reluctantly held back. Ju-Long strained her ears to listen in and passed on what she was hearing.

"A large section... about half of it gone. No one has been lost. Yet."

Beck glanced up at the sky.

"Is it the helicopter?" The bass throbbing of the rotors and engines shuddered through the jungle. It was unavoidable if they wanted its light – and potentially lethal too.

"Perhaps. Or it is just its time to fall."

"Still with most of the party on it," Beck said grimly. "Right."

He strode forward and crouched down at the cliff edge. No one blocked his way this time, now that the work had resumed.

"Mr Zhou!" he called.

"Beck! Hello!" Mr Zhou's voice came up from below.

"Does everyone need a stretcher? Is there anyone who could just climb up, if we gave them a rope?"

Ju-Long had tried this at the start of their adventure but the cliff had been too crumbly. That was why they had had to go down into the gorge. But if Beck remembered right, the cliff face here was rockier with less wet, soggy earth. It could be climbable, with a bit of assistance.

"One moment." A pause. "I count nine of us who could do so, including me."

It was almost half the party.

"Right!" Beck leapt to his feet. "Wait there!"

Well, duh, he thought, even as he hurried off. Wait there? What else are they going to do?

"Beck?" Ju-Long hurried after him, "There is no more rope."

"Not that we brought, no." He had found a vine-covered tree and he rummaged through the twining stalks until he found one of the right width – thick enough to hold a human's weight, thin enough to be flexible and act as rope. He tugged at it and it began to come away.

"You expect them to climb with a vine?"

"Why not? We did."

He measured the vine out between his outstretched arms, working it out as he went. He was about 160 centimetres tall, which meant there was the same distance between his fingertips if he held his arms out on either side. To cover a ten metre distance, there had to be six outstretched-arm-lengths of vine – plus some at the end, because he had to tie it to something somehow. The vine they had climbed with had been naturally anchored at the top of the cliff. This one was not.

It was long enough. He gathered it up in his hands and carried it to the cliff edge, next to the tripods.

"Coming down!" he called and threw it over, letting it unloop as it fell, while he held onto one end. Ju-Long spoke quickly to the rescue team leader as he gave Beck a sharp look. The man said a few grudging words and gave Beck a last, sideways look, before going back to his work.

"I told him this can only help," she said, "and he is from this province. He knows the strength of a good vine."

"Cool." Beck looped the far end of the vine around a tree, and threaded it into a giant clove hitch. What was left, he held on to. "Ask Mr Zhou to send the first one up."

A few moments later the vine grew taut. Beck held the vine and watched as the clove hitch knot bit tight.

He could never have done it on his own. The weight of the climber would probably have pulled him over the edge himself. But with the vine tied around the tree trunk taking the strain, it was working. He didn't have to pull the climber up – the climber could do that themselves, like he had, both hands on the thick, rough vine and walking themselves up the rock face. He just had to pray it would hold them.

"You could –" he grunted to Ju-Long, but she was already off, searching for another vine. Two vines, two ropes – they could cut the time it took to get the stranded trekkers off the ledge right down.

A head appeared at the end of Beck's vine – one of the Chinese Young Pioneer boys. He had to crawl over the edge himself, since Beck couldn't go to help him and all the rescue team were busy with the tripods. He gave Beck a smile and a friendly wave, then called down below. Immediately the vine went taut with another climber's weight.

On the other side of the tripods, Ju-Long threw a vine of her own down to the trekkers. Now there were four rescue lines going. Two that the trekkers could climb up, two with stretchers for the non-climbers. The number of stranded trekkers on the ledge was going down rapidly. Each one that made it up, on a stretcher or under their own steam, was led over to the medic for a check-up. Beck followed the rest of the action with half an eye, though he kept his concentration on the main task. As far as he could tell, only a couple were injured. But all of them were cold and hungry – which, Beck knew, could be just as lethal.

And then he felt joy surge in his heart as Mr Zhou's head appeared above the top of the cliff. The leader wouldn't have gone ahead of any of the young people – he had to be the last one up. He flashed Beck an enormous grin of relief and success, which Beck returned. Mr Zhou opened his mouth to say something –

The vine snapped, and Mr Zhou vanished from sight.

CHAPTER 35

The vine suddenly went slack. The broken end shot towards the cliff end, and stopped suddenly with a couple of metres to go.

"Mr Zhou!"

Beck lunged towards the edge, terrified of what he might see. Had Mr Zhou fallen back down to the ledge? Had he missed it and fallen into the gorge?

But no. The man was only a metre or so down, clinging onto the face of the cliff itself.

"Mr Zhou! Can you hold on?"

"I cannot much longer," Mr Zhou whispered through gritted teeth. Even as Beck watched, in horror, he could see Mr Zhou's grip on the cliff face slipping. The man spoke very calmly. "The rock is crumbling. If I move, it will probably go altogether. If I do not move, my weight will make it go anyway..."

His arms were outstretched and trembling with the effort. The ledge was several metres below him, but it was just a narrow sliver of ground. After that was nothing but the drop into the gorge.

He only had seconds. The rescuers with the tripods were still hauling up the last two stretchers. Ju-Long was the other side of them. The rescued trekkers were all gathered together with the medic –

"Grab the vine," Beck ordered. He plonked his backside onto the ground, digging both heels in and wrapping the vine's broken end around his clenched hands. There was no time to tie it again. That would take seconds, which Mr Zhou did not have.

"I will pull you off –" He heard Mr Zhou protest.

"Just grab it!" he shouted.

"My weight is too much –"

"*Do it!*" Beck bellowed. And then two things happened at once. He heard the crack and rattle of falling rock, and the vine dug sharply into his wrists and fingers as all Mr Zhou's weight fell on it, sharp enough to make him gasp and bite his lip against the pain.

And Mr Zhou had been right. Even though Beck was sitting down and braced against it, he could feel the weight pulling him. It wasn't his arms, it was his knees that were the weak point. He was holding the vine but it was his heels dug into the ground and his legs that were holding him in place. And his knees were going.

No. It was a simple refusal – an order to his body. Inside his head, he had gone back twenty-four hours. He was sitting beside the fire with Ju-Long and she was helping him find the ki inside him.

Then, the order had been to his arm. Now it was to his knees.

No. You will not move.

Your strength, and your will, combined, was how she had described it.

Ki. In his head he pictured all the energy of his body flowing into his legs.

And he felt his knees lock into place. They were like iron. They *would not* bend.

It only took a couple of seconds, but that was all that Mr Zhou needed as he swarmed up the vine. Then he was half onto solid ground, and others were running forward to grab him and haul him away from the edge.

At the same time the last two stretchers reached the top, one with a European boy and another with a Chinese girl.

The rescue was over.

Beck breathed out, emptying his lungs of air in a single sigh of relief. Then he slowly toppled over backwards and lay flat on his back, staring up at the sky. Beyond the lights of the helicopter, it was quite dark.

A beaming Mr Zhou and Ju-Long came to stand over him. Mr Zhou extended a hand and helped him climb to his feet.

"A thousand thank-yous," he said sincerely. "Without you and Ju-Long, we would still be there. And thank you for saving my life. I cannot believe you were able to hold me."

"Ju-Long taught me how." He grinned at Ju-Long. "I felt it. I felt it work."

"You would make a good pupil," she told him with a big smile. "And, I have to say, I have learned a great deal off you, too."

A shout went up: the rescue leader was gesturing at them to join the others. The rescue crew were dismantling the tripods, and the leader wanted them to get back to the landing point for pick-up before the jungle grew impenetrably dark. The three of them started to walk over.

"Well, we should hope for many more treks where you can continue to learn from each other," Mr Zhou commented. He was serious. "There will be complications because of what has happened. Inquests and enquiries. Many will want to cancel any further ventures like this. But we all talked about this, while we were on the ridge – we all want IYTO to continue. I think Mr Muller would too."

Beck and Ju-Long looked at each other.

"And so do we," Beck said. Ju-Long nodded in support. "We should all keep learning from each other. It's too important to cancel. And remember: the man who risks nothing, learns nothing."

"And the woman," Ju-Long added. Beck smiled and nodded.

"And the woman."

"Then we all agree. I will see what I can do to persuade the authorities as well. In the meantime – Beck, Ju-Long, we owe you so much. The other young people will go back to their families or be put in hotels until they can be reunited, but will you honour us by coming to stay in our house? My son Jian would love to meet you. We live on the coast. It will be peaceful and relaxing for a few days while everything is sorted out, and it is what you deserve."

They looked at each other in surprise.

"Well, thank you!" Beck said sincerely. "Thank you. I would love to."

He could certainly do with a break, and it certainly beat being stuck on the next plane back home.

"I will have to ask my family – but if they agree then yes, thank you," said Ju-Long. Mr Zhou beamed.

"Excellent! Well, we should go – we don't want the helicopter to leave us behind..."

They hurried after the rescuers, while Beck composed in his head the things he was going to have to say to Uncle Al.

"*Yeah, it all went well, apart from the landslide, the fatality, and us having to climb down a cliff and trek down a gorge to get help before certain disaster struck ... apart from all that it went like clockwork! And by the way, Mr Zhou would like me to stay over!*"

Beck smiled to himself. Oh yes, Uncle Al's face would be a picture.

But they had made it, and he and Ju-Long had helped pull off a truly remarkable rescue. And Beck felt he had made a friend for life.

Survival Tips

EATING IN THE JUNGLE

WARNING! ONLY TO BE USED IN EXTREME SITUATIONS!

PLANTS

Plants are a risky thing to eat in the jungle so there are a number of steps you must follow before you can eat a full mouthful of anything you find:

1. Smell it, if it smells like peaches throw it away; that familiar peachy smell is also the smell of cyanide.
2. Crush a small amount of it on the soft skin on the back of your wrist. If it's really bad for you then you will probably develop a rash there in a couple of minutes. If you do develop a rash wash it off fast with some water. If no rash appears, dab a little of it on your gums and wait for five minutes to see if it tingles or you develop sores.
3. Now you can actually chew some but spit out the plant matter and only swallow the liquid. After this you must wait eight hours without eating or drinking anything else.

4. If you feel fine you can eat a little more and wait another five hours.

5. Now you can eat a whole handful, again, seeing how you feel after twenty-four hours.

6. If you're still alive tuck in! It won't kill you!

ANT LARVAE

Ant Larvae contain more protein than beef pound for pound, so they are a great find when food and energy is running low. To extract the larvae, whittle a bamboo stick to a fine point and insert it into the nest as far as it will go. Keep a careful eye out for angry weaver ants as they have a particularly nasty sting. When you remove the stick from the nest it should be covered in larvae; simply pinch them off the stick and tuck in!

FROG

First check your frog over, if its brightly coloured it is probably poisonous, if it has warts it is a toad and they are toxic. Once you have established that it's safe to eat, push a knife into the back of its head to kill it. If the frog is big enough, you can skin it by making an incision down its back and pulling the skin off the meat, this should also take the guts away from the body too. Most of the meat is in the legs so hold the legs close to the fire until the meat is cooked through. On bigger frogs you can also find some breast meat, like the legs, just hold them in front of the fire until they are cooked.

Above all, remember: never, ever give up!

Bear Grylls has become known around the world as one of the most recognized faces of survival and outdoor adventure. His journey to this acclaim started in the UK, where his late father taught him to climb and sail.

Trained from a young age in martial arts, Bear went on to spend three years as a soldier in the British Special Forces, serving with 21 SAS. It was here that he perfected many of the skills that his fans all over the world enjoy watching him pit against mother-nature.

His popular survival TV shows include 'Man Vs Wild' and 'Born Survivor' which became one of the most watched programmes on the planet with an estimated audience of 1.2 billion. He has also hosted the hit adventure show 'Running Wild' on NBC, where he takes some of the world's best known movie stars on incredible adventures. Most recently US President Barrack Obama asked to appear on the show for a worldwide 'Running Wild Special'.

Bear is currently the youngest ever Chief Scout to the UK Scout Association and is an honorary Colonel to the Royal Marine Commandos.

He has authored 22 books, including the international number one Bestselling autobiography: *Mud, Sweat & Tears* and his hugely popular titles *Survival Guide for Life* and *True Grit*, a bestselling novel *Ghost Flight* and his *Mission Survival* fiction books which have sold over 4 million copies in China alone.

If you'd like to know more, please visit Bear's website, www.beargrylls.com where you can sign up for his most recent news, or follow him on Twitter, @BearGrylls, or on Facebook.

Also in this series

Mission Dragon

59520239R00105

Made in the USA
San Bernardino, CA
05 December 2017